HEART
of the Warrior

The Shadow Creek Ranch Series

HEART
of the Warrior

Charles Mills

REVIEW AND HERALD® PUBLISHING ASSOCIATION
HAGERSTOWN, MD 21740

Copyright © 1994 by
Review and Herald® Publishing Association

This book was
Edited by Raymond H. Woolsey
Designed by Patricia S. Wegh
Cover illustration by Joe Van Severen
Type set: 11.5/13.5 Century Book

PRINTED IN U.S.A.

99 98 97 96 95 94   10 9 8 7 6 5 4 3 2 1

R&H Cataloging Service
Mills, Charles Henning, 1950–
     Heart of the warrior.

          I. Title.
               813.54

ISBN 0-8280-0861-2

Dedication

To my wife, Dorinda,
in whose heart
I find my greatest joy.

Contents

CHAPTER 1

Racing the Wind

♈ ♈ ♈

Plenty?" The old man's voice carried across the bright, green-carpeted prairie as he strained to catch sight of any movement in the surrounding grassy fields.

"Plenty! This is no time to play games with me. Look to the south. The bus is coming. Don't you see it?"

Only the soft whisper of summer breezes echoed a response to the man's question.

"You'll like it in the mountains," he urged through wrinkled, age-worn hands cupped about his lips. "We might even see a bear. Or maybe a mountain lion. I've heard them often in the night."

He listened. There was no reply except the wind and the occasional thin-whistle call of a circling swainson's hawk.

"Come on, Plenty. You'll meet some very nice people, too. They're kind and they treat me with respect. Not like the others."

A large, sun-faded bus, pulling a tail of dust across

the flatlands, appeared over a small rise a quarter mile away. It began to slow when the driver spotted the old man waiting beside the road, battered suitcases and carefully rolled bundles at his feet.

"PLENTY! You must come now! The bus has arrived. It will not wait for you."

With a grind of gears and squeak of brakes, the vehicle lurched to a stop. The door swung open, revealing a smiling face perched high behind the steering wheel.

"Well, hello, Red Stone," the driver called with a friendly laugh. "You look like you've lost something."

The passenger-to-be nodded and pointed toward the prairie. "It's my great-granddaughter. Disappeared again. Can't find her."

"You mean Plenty?" the driver queried, glancing out across the tall grasses.

"Yes. I'm taking her with me to the mountains this summer. First time." Red Stone lifted a bundle and passed it to waiting hands at the top of the stairs. "At least, I thought I was."

The remainder of the suitcases were quickly stored in the noisy conveyance as the old man called out again and again. Still nothing moved beyond the dusty edges of the arrow-straight road.

"You'd better hop in," the driver urged. "I've got a schedule to keep." He paused. "Tell you what. Maybe this will get her attention." Reaching up, he gave a sharp tug on a chain hanging beside his head.

A sudden blast of air howled through twin horns mounted side by side on the top of the bus. An ear-piercing *blaaaat* screamed across the expanses on every side. The sound reverberated as it rolled through shallow gullies and surged over small rises in the treeless countryside.

By now, all eyes in the bus were searching the distant folds of the earth for any sign of the missing girl.

Suddenly someone called out, "There. To the west. I see something!" Passengers scurried from their seats and pressed sun-tanned faces against the cool glass that lined the side of the bus.

"Yes. I see her!" another shouted. "She's running . . . very fast." Mouths dropped open as one by one the group of travelers caught sight of a lone figure racing across the green carpet of prairie. The form seemed to flow as though it had no contact with the land. Tirelessly it ran northward, parallel to the road.

"Come on!" the driver shouted to the old man still waiting at the base of the steps. "We'll catch her up ahead."

Red Stone grabbed hold of the step rail as the bus lurched forward. He climbed hand over hand, fighting the power of the accelerating vehicle. Passengers cheered, and dust swirled behind rumbling tires.

The old man fought his way to an empty seat and grinned over at the driver. "You won't catch her," he said. "Nothing has ever been invented by a White man or Indian that can keep up with my Plenty."

The man at the wheel laughed as he threw his vibrating bus into high gear.

"She's like the wind," Red Stone continued.

Admiration filled his voice as he studied the distant figure that moved with unrestrained energy over the grasslands. "And you should see her shoot an arrow. State archery champion, you know. Beat out every White man who entered. The whole Crow tribe is proud of her."

"I remember," the driver nodded, holding tightly onto the steering wheel. His body swayed with the movement of the bus. "Our leaders say she'd make a fine warrior, if it were a hundred and fifty years ago, and if she was a boy." The man frowned. "'Course, if it were a hundred and fifty years ago, we wouldn't be stuck on this reservation and warriors could prove themselves in the hunt instead of in some state archery contest."

Red Stone shook his head. "Some things always remain the same," he called above the whine of the gears. "A true Crow Indian knows what he is inside. No government can take that away."

"You're dreaming again, Red Stone," the driver smiled. "But you're an old man. That's your privilege."

Passengers slid open their windows and leaned out into the slipstream of air. "Run, Plenty, run!" they shouted, their eyes watering from the wind in their faces. "Fly like the wind! FLY LIKE THE WIND!"

Plenty smiled to herself. She could see the bus racing along the ribbon of dirt and stone. She could see the arms waving, urging her on, faster and faster.

A narrow ditch flowed in her direction. She lengthened just one stride and slipped over it as easily as a hawk leaps a canyon.

The girl lowered her head a little and sped on, her legs pumping tirelessly, rhythmically, carrying her over the fields with a grace honed by many such runs, in years of racing the winds of southern Montana.

This is home, the girl told herself as a long-eared jackrabbit popped from his hole and glanced in her direction. Out there, beyond the boundaries of the reservation, were people who pointed and whispered, laughed, and turned their faces. But here by the banks of the Bighorn, at the foot of the Rosebud Mountains, along the endless expanses of prairie where fascinating creatures lived and the wind whistled encouragement to 14-year-old girls with hopes no one knew or understood, this was where her heart felt at home. Here she could run and leave the past far behind.

Plenty lifted her arms until they floated wing-like at her side. Oh, if she could only fly like the bird her people were named after. If only she could catch the currents of air racing up the distant mountain sides, she'd hover for hours like the eagle and the osprey. She'd call out her name and no one would laugh. For in the sky any name was beautiful.

But she had no wings, only arms. She couldn't fly, but she could run. She could run faster and faster until the world was a blur, and the only sound she could hear was the pounding of her own heart.

The girl smiled at the thought of the bus racing along beside her. She knew her great-grandfather was sitting inside the bus, watching. He understood why she raced along the prairie. He was wise. He knew secret things, things about the animals and about the earth, and about her.

Yes, she would go to the mountains with him, because he was old, and old was special to her people.

Plenty altered her course and began moving in a direction that would intercept the bus before it crossed the dry stream bed up ahead. She would do it for Great-grandfather. But her heart would stay on the prairie.

* * *

Five-year-old Samantha sat unmoving, staring at her dog, Pueblo. The animal, a mixture of most any canine you'd happen to meet, sat as still as a rock, staring at Samantha. They faced each other on the broad porch of the Station, their ranch home tucked in a beautiful valley amid the folds of the Gallatin National Forest.

The afternoon sun felt warm on their faces. In the bushes that surrounded the old, two-story, broad-beamed hotel, birds sang territorial songs and chased intruders away with chirps and squawks understood only by their own kind.

The hard winter was fast becoming a memory in the minds of those who lived on Shadow Creek Ranch. Not long ago, spring had finally arrived, loosening the icy grip the snow season had held on the land.

Flowers had bloomed with uncommon vigor as if believing their very presence would assure that no more storms would sweep down from the northwest and smother the mountains under deep blankets of white.

Now it was summer, and with it would come the guests everyone on the ranch had been eagerly awaiting and discussing.

A tan, muscular boy walked across the footbridge spanning the creek and made his way to the steps that led up to the porch. He paused when he saw his little dark-skinned, adopted sister sitting statue-like before her furry pet.

"Hi, Joey," the girl whispered, not moving her lips.

The young horse wrangler sat down heavily on the top stair and leaned against one of the thick posts that supported the second-floor deck.

"What are you doing?" the just-turned-17-year-old asked.

Samantha didn't move a muscle. "I'm training Pueblo," she whispered.

Joey nodded thoughtfully. "Training him to do what?"

"To stay," the little girl answered.

"Is it working?" Joey asked, a grin playing at the corners of his mouth.

"Oh, yes," Samantha said. "I just tell him to stay and then I sit really still like this. He doesn't move an inch as long as I stare at him."

Joey scratched his head. "But isn't the whole idea of making a dog stay so you can go somewhere and it won't follow?"

The little girl was silent for a long moment. "Maybe," she said quietly.

"Then aren't you training the dog just to stare at

you like some kinda statue?"

Samantha's head tilted slightly to one side. Pueblo's head tilted slightly in the same direction.

Samantha sighed. The dog sighed.

"I'm not doing this right," the little girl moaned.

Joey burst out laughing. "Oh, but you're teaching Pueblo something really neat."

"I am?"

"Sure, you're teaching him to play follow the leader. Not too many dogs know how to do that." Joey smiled at his companion. "Why, I'll bet if you go out to the pasture and run around the cottonwoods, that dog would follow you every step of the way."

"He would?" Samantha gasped. "Hey, that's pretty good, isn't it? I'm teaching my dog to play follow the leader." She jumped to her feet. Pueblo did the same. "Did you see that?" the girl squealed in glee. "I've taught Pueblo pretty good, don't you think?"

"Sure do," Joey said as he rose and walked to the front door. "You're the best dog teacher in Montana."

Samantha fairly burst with excitement. "Watch this," she said. Facing the dog she commanded, "Pueblo, follow me!"

The youngster raced down the steps and headed for the footbridge. Pueblo barked enthusiastically and followed at his young owner's heels.

"Good dog, good dog!" Joey heard Samantha call. "Just wait till I show Wendy and Debbie. They'll be amazed!"

The boy chuckled to himself and glanced up toward the towering mountains that ringed the ranch. Yes, summer had definitely arrived and he wasn't sorry. Not one bit.

"What's all the commotion about?" a voice called from the balcony just over the Station's front door. Joey saw Mr. Hanson step from his office on the second floor, file folder in hand.

"Samantha is teaching Pueblo to follow her everywhere she goes," Joey announced. He stuck his head through the kitchen door and filled his nostrils with the odor of freshly baked bread.

"Doesn't that mutt kinda do that anyway?" the man called from above.

"Yeah, but before, he didn't know he was supposed to," Joey laughed as he headed for the den. "Have you seen Grandpa Hanson?"

The man paused before reentering his office, from where he was constantly connected by fax and phone lines to his company headquarters in New York City. "He went into Bozeman a couple hours ago to pick up Red Stone at the bus station. Should be back around supper. Whatcha need?"

Joey sighed. "I can't find those new saddle blankets—you know, the fancy ones we ordered from Utah."

The man's face appeared above the railing. "What do I know from saddle blankets? I'm a lawyer. I work with computers. They don't leave stuff lying around to step in. I kinda like that."

Joey laughed. "Maybe Wendy's got 'em."

"Now there's a possibility," Mr. Hanson nodded. "Do try to leave her in one piece if she is involved in this latest mystery. She's my daughter and I love her."

Joey waved and headed for the door. "Not to fear, Mr. H. Me and Wendy are best of friends."

"That'll be the day," the lawyer chuckled as he entered his large work room and settled once again before the screen of his powerful computer.

"Wendy?" Joey called, his eyes searching the distant pasture. He saw a horse and rider emerge from behind a stand of trees at the far end of the orchard. "Hey, Wendy. I want to talk to you."

The rider waved and steered her mount down the long driveway that led from the old logging road half a mile away to the Station.

As the pair drew closer, Joey blinked. The blanket tucked neatly between the saddle and the smooth, muscular back of the animal looked strangely familiar. It also looked brand-new.

"I don't believe it," Joey said angrily when Wendy reigned her horse to a stop beside him. "You took one of the new blankets right out of the tack house without even asking me. Those are supposed to be for the mares arriving tomorrow, part of our summer herd."

"So? I just tried it out for you," the girl shrugged. "Big deal."

Joey bit his tongue.

"Besides," Wendy continued, "Early really, really likes this blanket. He says it feels so soft on his back, like velvet."

"Listen, Miss Soft-Like-Velvet," Joey retorted, "you can tell this pitiful excuse for a horse that her old

18

blanket is still plenty good enough. If she has a problem with that, I'll find a nice, big piece of *sandpaper* for you guys to use from now on. Understand!?"

Wendy lifted her chin. "Good grief, Joey. Who died and left you king of the universe?"

"Wrangler Barry, that's who," the boy responded firmly. "Well, he didn't exactly die, but being buried under 12 feet of snow in his wrecked truck with Debbie for three days ain't exactly what I call living."

Wendy swallowed hard. "That scared 10 years off my life, and when you're only 11, that's a lot."

Joey nodded. "Well, Barry's comin' out soon and I want to have everything ready when he gets here. So get my new blanket off that crazy, do-everything-before-everyone-else-does-it horse of yours and don't make a mess in the barn while you're at it."

"OK, OK!" Wendy scowled as she gave Early a gentle kick and started across the footbridge. "Hey, are you sure Barry can work here this summer?" she asked as Joey fell in beside her. "I mean, doesn't he have to use a cane and stuff? Doctors said it'll be a long time before his insides heal."

Joey shrugged. "He's supposed to take it easy and not do any ridin' or liftin' of heavy stuff, like feed sacks and saddles."

"What else does a wrangler do all day?" the young rider asked.

Joey rolled his eyes. "Give me a break, Wendy Hanson," he groaned. "You know how hard we work to keep the ranch livestock healthy and safe. There're lots of jobs he can do. I'll just make sure he doesn't strain himself. After all, he's still the boss, even if he is in bad shape. You'd be using a cane, too, if you had a steering column jammed into your chest at 50 miles an hour."

"Ouch," the girl responded, with a shudder. "Let's not talk about what happened anymore. Makes me feel creepy inside."

"Fine with me," Joey agreed. "Let's just talk about people who steal new saddle blankets." The two continued through the pasture gate and made their way to the horse barn. It would be hard to forget the pain of what happened when the snows came early, especially after Wrangler Barry arrived. His disability would serve as a constant reminder of the fearful days and agonizing nights they'd all experienced.

* * *

Debbie cringed as the physical therapist lifted the patient's right arm slowly, ever so slowly, until it hovered just above his head. "That's one more inch today," the woman wearing the white smock encouraged. "I knew you could do it."

Barry's face was red from the exertion and his breathing came in quick, painful bursts. Debbie watched a tear form at the corner of her friend's eye and slip down his pale cheek.

"That's more than last week," the therapist said, triumphantly. "I'm proud of you, Barry Gordon." She gently lowered the arm to the wrangler's lap. "We're experiencing real improvement here. We'll have you back roping calves and riding bulls in short order." She scribbled some notations on her clipboard.

"Yeah, right," Barry said without emotion, his eyes closed. He waited for the pain to subside.

Debbie smiled and touched the young man's shoulder. "It *was* higher than last time," she said."

"So after eight weeks of agony I'll be able to raise my hand above my head." Barry slipped his arm into the sling that hung loosely from his neck. "Forgive me if I don't throw a party."

"These things take time," the therapist interjected. "Any improvement is a good sign."

The horseman stood and leaned heavily on the stout, wooden cane that had become his constant companion during the four months since he had left the hospital. "I think it's time I face facts," he said coldly. "I've got a useless leg and a useless arm. Period. I can come in here every week and you can put me through your series of Chinese tortures, but it's not going to change anything." He turned toward the door. "For someone who wants to run a ranch someday, being half a man isn't going to cut it." He glanced at Debbie.

"Mr. Gordon," the therapist called out, her voice a little louder than usual. "You had an accident. The steering column of your truck just about broke you into two pieces. You had severe damage to internal organs, your rib cage was crushed, and vital nerve paths were interrupted. I think you should be happy just to be alive."

"Oh, you do?" Barry spun around and moved

menacingly toward the speaker. "Maybe *you* need to learn something. Alive doesn't mean being able to breathe and blink your eyes." Debbie stepped forward but Barry pushed her back against the file cabinet, causing its collection of bottles to clatter against each other and tumble across the metal shelves. "For your information, I'm not alive. I'm dead. When I wake up in the morning and have to have someone help me get out of bed, I'M DEAD! When I try to write my name, and the letters look like they were scribbled by a 3-year-old, I'M DEAD! And when I see my horses running through the north pasture and I can't go along for the ride, I'm as dead as you can get without someone tossing you into the ground and putting a stone over your head.

"You want to help me? Huh?" The wrangler pressed his body against the therapist, pushing her into the wall. "Then get a gun, put it to the side of my head, and pull the trigger so my brain can be as dead as my body. That would be a real improvement. Do you understand?"

"Stop it!" Debbie screamed. "Stop it, Barry. She's just trying to help. We all are."

The young man backed away as sudden sobs shook his thin, bent frame. "I . . . I can't even dream anymore," he moaned. "There's no future for me. No ranch. No horses. Nothing." He turned and faced Debbie. "No one wants half a man."

Debbie glanced at the therapist, who nodded and quickly slipped from the room. As the door closed, the girl moved slowly to her friend's side and placed her arms around his trembling shoulders. She held him for a long moment until his sobs quieted. Then she lifted his chin and gazed into his eyes. "You listen to me, cowboy," she said softly. "You saved my life that night. Even though you were terribly hurt, you took care of me. You pushed that pipe up through the snow so we could have air to breathe. You were so gentle, so caring. Half of Barry Gordon is a whole lot more than *all* of many guys. Do you hear me?"

The wrangler closed his eyes and a painful sigh escaped his lips. "I . . . I wish I could believe that," he whispered. "I really do."

Debbie sat down on the examining table. "Look. You're moving out to Shadow Creek Ranch so I can keep an eye on you. Joey's been counting the days. Even Wendy said she's willing to tolerate you for another summer." A tiny smile lifted the corners of the young man's mouth. "So the only thing you have to *be* this summer is there, with us, with the family who thinks you're the best wrangler in all of Montana."

Debbie waited as her words filtered through the pain that surrounded her friend like a thick, dark curtain.

Barry nodded. "OK," he said. "Maybe I can at least bug Wendy for a few weeks. That'll be fun."

Debbie grinned. "There, you see? Life *is* worth living after all."

The wrangler stood to his feet. "Man, you give a girl a driver's license and she thinks she's Mother Teresa."

"That's right," Debbie nodded as she helped her companion toward the door. "Someone's gotta take care of all the recovering cowboys of the world. This summer, you're at the top of my list."

The two exited, leaving the room silent except for the drip . . . drip . . . drip of spilled liquids escaping the broken bottles in the metal cabinet by the window.

* * *

Lizzy Pierce and Grandma Hanson were sitting on the front porch peeling potatoes when they heard the sound of an approaching automobile.

"Must be your husband with Red Stone," Lizzy said, looking up toward the road that ran above and beside the stately, white Station. "It'll be nice to have the old Indian up there on Freedom Mountain again. Kids love him, and I like his stories about the history of his people."

With a grind of gears, the farm truck turned and rattled up the valley toward the Station, dust swirling about its old, paint-chipped body.

Grandma squinted, then opened her eyes wide in surprise. "I see *three* people in there," she gasped. "Not two."

"You're right," her companion agreed. "Maybe Red Stone was able to talk his great-granddaughter into spending the summer with him on the mountain."

The women rose, brushed off their aprons, and descended the broad steps just as the truck bounced to a halt in its usual parking spot beneath a tall spruce.

"Hello, ranch-type people," a strong, male voice called from the cab. "We come in peace for all mankind."

Grandma Hanson rolled her eyes. "My husband, the astronaut. Get out of that truck, old man, and introduce us to the young lady sitting beside you."

The three clamored from the vehicle and gathered by the front grill. "Red Stone says he wants to do the honors," Grandpa Hanson announced.

The old Indian cleared his throat. English was not an easy language for him. Never had been. It was a far cry from the guttural, almost German-like sounds of his native Crow.

"This my great-granddaughter," he said proudly. "She come with me to Freedom Mountain. Her name is Plenty Crops Growing, but I just say Plenty."

The young girl with the long black hair and dark eyes lifted her chin. "You heard right. My name is Plenty Crops Growing. So you can laugh if you want."

Red Stone spoke a few quick words in Crow then continued. "My great-granddaughter named by tribal council. Usually uncle or aunt gives name to child at birth. But when Plenty was born, there no close relative, so council give name."

Lizzy reached out her hand. "Hello, Plenty," she said. "We're glad you'll be our neighbor this summer."

Plenty stepped back just a little. "My great-grandfather talked me into coming. I didn't want to. This is the White man's world."

Red Stone spoke sharply again, his words understood only by the girl. Plenty nodded. "Thank you for picking us up at the bus station," she said softly. "We'll be going now."

"Won't you stay for supper?" Grandma Hanson urged. "We've got beans baking in the oven. Fresh bread, too. You're certainly welcome to stay. We'll drive you up to the mountain after the dishes are done."

The girl unconsciously licked her lips. She *was* hungry. The trip from the reservation had taken most of the day. She'd only had an apple and small bag of cashew nuts to eat since leaving her prairie home.

Turning to her great-grandfather, she spoke in Crow. The old man nodded enthusiastically. "We'll stay," the girl announced. "But only until after supper."

"Great!" Grandma Hanson responded happily. "Come, you can help us finish peeling the potatoes while Grandpa Hanson and Red Stone load provisions into the truck."

"I'm not your slave," Plenty said flatly, not moving.

"Oh, heaven's no," the old woman called over her shoulder. "But you are going to be our neighbor. And around here, neighbors help each other." She stopped and turned, a smile lighting her face. "It's the White man's way on Shadow Creek Ranch. You'll get use to it."

Plenty blinked and stared at the woman wearing the colorful apron. "Come on, now," Grandma Hanson encouraged. "We need to hurry. The others will be arriving soon, and on this ranch meals are a big thing. If they're not on the table when they're supposed to be . . . well . . . it's not a pretty sight."

With that she continued toward the front porch. Plenty looked at Red Stone, who just shrugged and ambled off beside Grandpa Hanson.

Lizzy stepped forward, a gentle smile on her face. "I'm from New York, Plenty," she said. "It took me a little while to adjust to Shadow Creek Ranch, too. Mrs. Hanson's right. You'll get used to it."

Plenty studied the woman thoughtfully. "You don't mind that I'm an Indian?" she asked.

Lizzy shrugged. "Not if you don't mind that I'm from East Village."

The girl looked out over the pasture and to the mountains beyond. Late afternoon shadows lay long across the forests and meadows. The ringing melody of Shadow Creek filtered through the songs of birds and buzz of unseen insects. "It's not like the prairie," she said softly.

"Tell me about your home," Lizzy invited, slipping her hand around Plenty's arm and urging her toward the Station.

The young Indian brushed long strands of black hair from her eyes. "I, uh . . . I live in Pryor, in a little trailer with my mom and dad. He works for the coal company."

As the two made their way across the green lawn, Red Stone turned and looked over his shoulder. He smiled, then continued in the direction of the shed that stood at the back of the big way station.

* * *

As predicted, activity about the ranch increased considerably as suppertime approached. First, Debbie and Wrangler Barry arrived amid much tooting of horns and shouts of welcome. The cowboy found himself the center of attention, with Grandpa and Grandma Hanson, their lawyer son Tyler, and Lizzy making over him like a long-lost relative.

Even Red Stone had heard of the accident and he joined in the welcome with his share of smiles and back-patting.

Plenty remained on the porch, watching the reunion until Lizzy insisted she come down and meet Debbie and her friend.

Joey, who'd been riding his horse, Tar Boy, miles away from Shadow Creek Ranch, suddenly appeared. He thundered full-speed down the long driveway, waving his hat in the air; a joyous grin lit his sun-tanned face.

"Hey, Barry!" he shouted as his large, black stallion skidded to a halt. The boy hopped off as easily as a frog from a lily pad. "Man, am I glad to see you. You're looking great!"

Barry lifted his cane and smiled weakly. "Hey, Joey. How's the herd?"

"Ornery as ever," came the happy reply. "And if one of those new saddle blankets looks a little used, blame Wendy, not me. She stole it when I—" The boy paused when he saw Plenty standing beside Lizzy.

"Who are you?" he asked abruptly.

Plenty jumped as the young rider's attention

suddenly landed on her.

Lizzy grinned and whispered. "Don't mind him. He's from New York, too."

"I'm Red Stone's great-granddaughter," the girl said. "Who are you?"

Now it was Joey's time to be nervous. "I . . . I'm Joey Dugan. You're an Indian, aren't you?"

"Yes. Crow. You know, the people you White folks took this land from."

Lizzy quickly stepped forward. "Why don't we all head inside while Joey takes Barry's things to the horse barn? Supper's almost ready."

Joey stared at Plenty, then shook his head. "I didn't take nothin' from anybody," he said flatly. "So don't worry about it."

Debbie lifted her hand. "Say, Plenty, I like that shirt you're wearing. Did you make it yourself?"

"My mother did. She sews."

"I thought so," the older girl gasped. "You just can't find hand-stitching like that in stores nowadays, even at the mall." She slipped her arm around the Indian and led her away from the group. "I sew, too," everyone heard her say. "Well, not a lot of hand-stitching, but I'd like to learn."

Joey looked about, then lifted his hands. "Hey, what's her problem?"

Red Stone stepped forward. "Plenty have anger inside. She no like White man."

"There's a few White men I ain't too fond of, either," Joey countered.

"No," Red Stone continued. "Plenty not like *all*

29

White man. She say they robbed Crow of land many years ago."

The young boy nodded slowly. "I guess that's sorta true."

"She need to learn lesson," the old Indian sighed. "Maybe I teach her this summer. I try."

Joey was silent as he and Wrangler Barry headed over the footbridge toward the barn. When he spoke his words were somber.

"Did you see the way she looked at me? It was like she hated me, and I don't even know her." He paused. "I mean, I've had guys back in New York who didn't like me, but that's 'cause I gave 'em grief—you know, messed with 'em. But Plenty hates me and I ain't done nothin' to her."

Barry leaned heavily on his cane as he walked. "It's not about you. It's about stuff that happened a long time ago, before you or I, or even Grandpa Hanson, were born."

"You mean, how the government took away their lands so the pioneers could build farms and ranches? Lizzy told me about that last winter in home-school history class. She said the White man sorta took over the whole country, even though the Indians were here first."

The older wrangler nodded and sighed. "Yup. That's what it's about. Plenty, like many in her tribe, and most other tribes for that matter, grow up hearing about how the White man spoiled everything. It's a very old hatred that's reborn with each new generation."

Joey reached up and unlatched the big wooden door that led into the horse barn. "But I wasn't there. I didn't do nothin' to the Crow, or Flathead, or Chippewa, or Cree—those Montana Indian tribes I read about."

Barry hobbled inside as Joey unloaded his burden of suitcases and a sleeping bag onto the narrow cot by the worktable under the window. "Think about it," the horseman said, rubbing his ribs gently. "How would you feel if you knew that many, many years ago your great-great-great-grandfather rode into Plenty's great-great-great-grandfather's village and killed women and children, burned down the tents, took the horses, and carried the surviving men off to prison, simply because the tribe insisted that they had a right to live on that particular plot of land?"

Joey kicked at a piece of straw. "I'd feel kinda lousy about that."

"Well, let's just say Plenty is feeling lousy about that too, every morning when she gets up and sees her once-proud people stuck on a reservation. She doesn't know who to blame, so she takes it out on Joey Dugan, and Barry Gordon, and Lizzy Pierce—anyone she sees whose skin is white."

The teenager nodded slowly. "So, what am I supposed to do?"

"Beats me," Barry said, slowly opening the first suitcase and eyeing its contents. "You can't do anything about the past. It's the present you have to worry about." The older wrangler smiled a weak smile and looked out through the open door. "Did I just sound like Debbie?"

"I do that sometimes, too," Joey said thoughtfully. "Scary, ain't it?"

Barry shook his head and chuckled. "Let's get me settled in. I think I smell supper coming from the Station. We'll talk about Indians . . . and other stuff . . . a little later, OK?"

Joey smiled. "Man, I'm glad you're here. Summer on Shadow Creek Ranch just wouldn't be the same without you."

"Yeah," the wrangler nodded, suddenly sad. "It wouldn't be the same."

The horseman walked to the open door and studied the distant patch of cottonwoods at the far end of the pasture. He could see the ranch's herd of horses grazing contentedly on the sweet, summer grasses.

Joey sat down and looked at his friend and mentor for a long moment. "We'll make it work," he said softly. "Don't worry about it, OK?"

"You mean Plenty?"

Joey nodded. "That, too," he said.

CHAPTER 2

Rainbow Trout

What's that?" Mr. Hanson asked, looking up from his book. His father had guided a heavily loaded cart into the den and pushed it to the center of the room.

Evening crickets chirped and buzzed outside as the inhabitants of Shadow Creek Ranch rested in their favorite spots about the large, cozy chamber.

Grandpa Hanson leaned one arm on the over-sized box and read the name written across the top. "Says here, 'Please deliver to David Jarboe in care of Shadow Creek Ranch, Montana.'"

"Who?" the children chorused.

The old man smiled. "David Jarboe. He's one of the five guests arriving tomorrow. Return address is Seattle, Washington. Seems my conversation with the police chief of that city last summer paid off."

Wendy arose and ambled over to the mysterious crate. "What's in it?" she asked, eyeing the "Handle With Care" stickers plastered all over the sides and top. "Must be something fragile—or dangerous."

"Down, girl," Mr. Hanson called to his youngest daughter. "Unless your name is David Jarboe, you've got no business snooping around that box. We'll let the boy open it himself when he gets here."

Wendy bent and knocked softly on the wooden slats. "Maybe it's a secret government project that the FBI wants smuggled to Montana so they can test it up in the mountains where no one will see."

Debbie rolled her eyes, then returned to her fashion magazine. "And maybe it's none of your business," she sighed.

Joey stretched tired muscles. "When's the plane arriving?" he asked through a broad yawn.

"Two o'clock sharp," Grandpa Hanson announced. "Ms. Cadena says she'll be there to meet the group and bring them out to the ranch in her van."

All eyes turned to Mr. Hanson. The lawyer looked up sharply. "What?" he asked, spreading his hands.

Debbie smiled. "It'll be nice to have Ms. Cadena out here more often. I've missed her."

Tyler Hanson glanced at his daughter. "Yes, it will," he said matter-of-factly. "As the director of Project Youth Revival, she's a welcome addition to our summer family."

"Oh, brother," Wendy chuckled. "Such formality. She wouldn't happen to be the reason why you bought that new bottle of cologne the other day, would she?"

"Children, children," Mr. Hanson sighed, shaking his head slowly from side to side. "When a man buys a new bottle of cologne it doesn't necessarily mean he's trying to attract the attention of a member of the opposite sex."

"What's it called?" Wendy queried.

Mr. Hanson cleared his throat. "The name of this particular product is . . . 'Mr. Macho.'"

Debbie giggled, then suppressed her outburst. "No, no. You're not trying to attract Ms. Cadena. You just want Tar Boy and Early to think you smell nice."

The lawyer reddened. "I like the aroma of Mr. Macho. Besides, Ruth . . . I mean, Ms. Cadena and I are just friends. She's a warm, intelligent woman with whom I enjoy conversing from time to time."

Grandma Hanson shifted her position and studied her fingernails. "You two sure did a lot of conversing out on the footbridge last spring. One of you must be hard of hearing 'cause you were standing so close together. Shocked me so much I almost dropped my binoculars."

Mr. Hanson lifted his hands. "Such privacy I have on this ranch. Dad? Were you spying on me, too?"

"Couldn't," the old man grinned. "She had my binoculars."

The room erupted with laughter as Mr. Hanson staggered to his feet. "Some parents you are, and in front of the kids!"

"The children were nowhere to be seen," the man's father urged.

"Yeah," Joey agreed. "You don't think we'd sink so low as to spy on you and Ms. Cadena with binoculars, do you? Besides. We didn't need 'em. We could see just fine from the bushes."

The lawyer sank back into his chair. "I live in a fishbowl," he moaned. "Can't even have a quiet conversation with a pleasant woman without the whole Station getting involved."

His mother reached over and patted his hand. "That's the price you pay for being Mr. Macho," she whispered.

Grandpa Hanson settled into his chair by the fireplace and slipped a piece of paper from his shirt pocket. "And, speaking of Ms. Cadena," he said when the giggles had died down, "she gave me this list of names, along with a short description of our guests. If we can stop teasing my son long enough, I'll tell you what she wrote."

Wendy walked over and sat down on her father's lap. She curled up into a ball and pressed her head against the man's chest as Mr. Hanson began stroking her soft, blond hair. "Don't listen to those guys, Daddy," she said softly. "It's OK if you want to talk to Ms. Cadena on the footbridge. She's nice."

"Well, thank you, Wendy," Mr. Hanson responded.

The girl paused. "Are you wearing Mr. Macho right now?"

"Yes, I am."

Wendy closed her eyes. "I like it. Makes you smell like Early."

Debbie's hand shot to her mouth as Mr. Hanson blinked. His youngest daughter snuggled even closer and sighed contentedly. "Thank you . . . again," the young lawyer said, realizing that Wendy's comment, as strange as it sounded, really was meant to be a compliment. He knew there was nothing as important to the little girl resting in his lap as her mare, Early. In this particular case, smelling like a horse was something any father could be proud of.

"As I was saying," Grandpa Hanson continued, trying to keep his own composure, "we're going to have five teens as our guests this summer. Here's what Ms. Cadena says about each one.

"First there's Gina McClintock, from Rochester, New York. She's 14 years old, likes to read books about old trains, has a pet fish called Fin, and was arrested three times for shoplifting and once for setting fire to her high school science lab."

Lizzy shook her head. "Oh, dear. Sounds like someone I used to know." She shot a quick glance in Joey's direction.

The boy grinned. "Ah, the good old days," he said.

"Then there's Alex Slater, 15, enjoys watching baseball games on TV, likes making model airplanes, and is writing a book entitled *How to Get Rich Without Leaving the Comfort of Your Own Cell.* He's been in San Francisco juvenile detention seven times for fencing stolen goods, misuse of the telephone system, destroying public property, and picketing outside City Hall without a permit." The man paused. "There's a note here that says, 'Alex has real potential.'"

"There's that word again," Joey chuckled.

Grandpa Hanson adjusted his reading glasses.

"Then we have David Jarboe. He's coming to us from Seattle. It says here he's 16, likes nature, enjoys reading about wildlife safaris in Africa, and was arrested for stealing an alligator."

"An alligator?" the children chorused.

"That's what it says. He's also been detained for disturbing the peace, invasion of privacy, loitering, and shoplifting."

"Hey, he likes nature," Debbie called out. "I can have him help me with our hikes. Maybe he knows about those weird flowers at the foot of Mount Blackmore. I can't figure out what they are."

"Maybe so," the old man agreed. "Then there're two other kids from Dallas, Texas; Lyle Burns, 16, and Judy Chisko, 14. They're cousins who like to give the police a hard time. Haven't done anything really crazy, but the chief down there thought a few weeks in Montana might do them some good. Sorta head them in a new direction. We'll see."

Lizzy sighed. "Innocent children who've lost their way. It's a shame, really, that there has to be a program like Project Youth Revival. Wouldn't it be nice if all teenagers had happy homes with moms and dads who loved them? Sure would cut out a lot of pain and suffering from the process of growing up."

Grandma Hanson nodded. "I'm glad there're people like Ruth Cadena who've dedicated their lives to helping wayward teens. I'm also glad we can have a little part in what she and her organization are trying to do."

"Me, too," Debbie and Joey agreed.

"How 'bout you, Wendy?" Mr. Hanson queried. "Think we're up to the task?"

Everyone looked in the lawyer's direction and found the normally energetic 11-year-old fast asleep in her father's arms.

"They always look so sweet like this," Mr. Hanson whispered. "Even Wendy."

Joey chuckled. "Don't be fooled. I'll bet she's cooking up some mischief between snores."

Debbie nodded. "Probably planning something diabolical, something that will send her off on another great adventure like finding bones in the attic or discovering an old, abandoned farmhouse in the mountains. There's only one Wendy, that's for sure."

Mr. Hanson smiled as he bent and kissed the sleeping cheek. "Life would be far too boring around here without her."

The crickets continued their late-night sonnets as the man slowly rocked back and forth. His arms encircled the young girl who, despite her strong-willed ways and wild imagination, was deeply loved by all who lived on Shadow Creek Ranch.

* * *

"What time is it?" Joey stood gazing out from the horse barn, a pitchfork in one hand and a bale of straw dangling from the other.

Wrangler Barry laid down the leather strap he was attempting to fashion into a halter and glanced at his watch. "It's about five minutes from the last time you asked," he said.

"Then it's almost 3:30, right?"

"Right."

The boy nodded. "Should be here any minute. Can't wait to meet our new guests. I wonder what they're like."

The older wrangler picked up the strap once again and started carefully cutting along one edge. "Oh, they probably have two feet and two hands and two eyes and—"

"You know what I mean," Joey chuckled. "I wonder if they'll like it out here."

"What's not to like?" Barry asked without looking up. "We've got mountains and creeks and horses and Grandma Hanson's vegetable stew and—"

"You're right," the teenager nodded. "They'll love it." He paused. "I sure wouldn't want to move back to New York City. I'm glad Mr. H let me come west with him. Me and Sam are never going to leave this ranch for as long as we live."

"No, sir," a faint, female voice called from somewhere overhead. "I'm going to stay here until I have as many wrinkles as Lizzy. Maybe even more."

Wrangler Barry and Joey glanced about the dusty, sun-lit room. "Sam?" Joey called. "Where are you?"

"Up on the roof," came the distant reply.

The two horsemen stumbled out of the barn and looked along the slanted surface covering the structure. There, sitting high atop the ridge of the roof was Samantha, her slender arms hugging a metal lightning rod that jutted into the cloudless sky.

"What on earth are you doing up there?" Joey called out, concern in his voice. "You might fall and break every bone in your scrawny little body."

The girl giggled. "Then the doctor can fix me up like he did Wrangler Barry."

"I wouldn't wish that on anyone," the older horseman moaned with a painful grin. "Why don't you come down so we won't have to bother the good doctor today, OK?"

Samantha tightened her grip on the lightning rod. "But I'm watching for Ms. Cadena's van. I wanna be the first to see it."

"Come on, Sam," Joey urged. "We'll watch for it together, down here, where it's safe."

The little girl hesitated, then suddenly stiffened. "Wait," she called. "I see it. I SEE IT!" Samantha let go of the pole and pointed wildly to the west. "It's coming around the cor—"

In her excitement, the speaker forgot where she was. Her body swayed forward, then backward. Then she lost her balance and began sliding down the roof.

Joey shouted, "Samantha, grab something!" but the little form continued to pick up speed as it careened along the smooth, metal surface.

In an instant, Joey was running toward the spot where he calculated his sister would hit the ground. Samantha sailed out into space at the same instant that Joey hurled himself forward, his arms outstretched. They met in mid-air with a resounding *thump*. The impact sent Joey, with the little girl held tightly in his arms, flipping end over end through the open barn door.

The two landed hard against the bale of straw the young wrangler had been holding moments before.

Joey's right leg slammed into the pitchfork that lay beside the bale. The long tool flew straight up, spinning slowly around and around.

Since gravity is as effective in Montana as anywhere else in the world, what goes up must come down. The teenager saw the pointed ends of the pitchfork dropping straight for his head. He had time to shift his position just enough to allow the tool to embed itself with a *twang* deep into the hard-packed earth inches from his face.

Samantha lay very still for a long moment, then opened her eyes. She looked at her brother, then at the pitchfork. After letting out a frustrated sigh she announced, "Man, I'm not going up on the roof again. Getting up's easy. But comin' back down sure is a lot of work."

With that she raced out of the corral and headed for the footbridge, anxious to meet the soon-to-arrive vehicle.

Barry ambled over to where his friend lay sprawled across the barn floor. He studied the pitchfork, which still swayed from its collision with the ground. "You wanted to know when the van was coming," he said. "Well, it's here." Then, with a smile, he added, "You might want to freshen up a bit. I think you're lying in horse poop."

Joey grinned. "Is that what that smell is? I

thought it was Mr. H's new cologne."

Barry laughed as he watched his friend and roommate stumble to his feet. "That was quite a catch," he said.

The younger boy rubbed his elbow. "Remind me to put Sam on a diet. No more peach jam for her." Then, with a chuckle and a shake of his head, he headed for the washbasin.

Ms. Cadena carefully guided her fully-loaded van down the long driveway to the front of the Station. Inside, eager eyes gazed ahead, trying to drink in the incredible beauty of the valley and mountains surrounding it.

"Do they think we're criminals?" a voice called from the back section of the vehicle.

Ms. Cadena smiled. "They know you've all made some bad choices. Who hasn't?"

The driver saw a group of people gathering at the base of the front porch steps. "They also know that people can change if they want to. That's why this place exists—to give you an opportunity to choose a different course for your life, preferably one on the legal side of the law."

The woman stuck her hand out the window and waved. "Give 'em a chance, OK?" she encouraged. "They work hard to show you a good time."

"I've been to rehab joints before," the voice said flatly.

"Not like this one," Ms. Cadena grinned. "There's only one Shadow Creek Ranch."

The van slowed to a stop and was immediately

surrounded by smiling faces. The driver opened the door and hopped out. "Come on, you guys. The fun's out here, not in the van."

The side door slid open and a group of young, self-conscious teenagers tumbled out into the bright sunlight.

Joey and Wrangler Barry joined the group just as Ms. Cadena was beginning introductions. "This is Gina," she announced, pointing to a slender, brown-haired girl with rosy cheeks; blue eyes peered from under a train conductor's cap. She wore striped overalls and a pair of thick-tongued athletic shoes.

"Where'd you get that neat cap?" Debbie asked as she approached the girl."

I went for a ride on a steam train once," Gina said shyly. "They had 'em at the souvenir shop."

"I like it," the older girl said warmly. "Nice over-alls, too."

"Thanks," the new guest responded.

"Makes her look like Casey Jones," a voice called from the van. Joey peered inside, his eyes opening wide with surprise.

"What're you looking at, cowboy?" the voice asked. "Ain't you ever seen someone in a wheelchair before?"

"That's Alex," the tall, blond-haired boy standing beside Gina volunteered. "Watch out for him. He'll rip off your last dollar as fast as you can say 'con man.'"

"Now, David," the voice chuckled. "You're turning the whole group against me before they've even had a chance to find out what a wonderful guy I am. If someone will give me a hand, I'll get out of this rolling cattle car and down to business."

Joey and Mr. Hanson reached in and carefully lowered a wheelchair and its occupant to the ground. "There. That's better," the seated teenager said with a smile, his dark eyes scanning the gathering as if looking for something. Curly black hair stood out from his scalp like a forest of crooked pine trees.

"Hello?" he called, catching sight of Debbie. "Babe alert!" He wheeled himself toward the surprised girl. "How 'bout you and me headin' for the pasture to look for wildflowers?"

"How 'bout if you go by yourself and find a poison mushroom?" Debbie responded nonthreateningly.

"Don't play hard to get," the boy pressed. "You know you like me. I can see it in those beautiful eyes of yours. Besides, I've got money. Cold, hard cash. Lots of it."

Wrangler Barry limped to Debbie's side. "Take it easy, hotshot," he said. "I happen to know that this . . . *babe* . . . might be a little more than you bargained for. Why don't you pick on someone your own size, like that vision of beauty standing over there?" He pointed at Wendy. "I happen to know she doesn't have a steady boyfriend at the present."

Wendy looked Alex straight in the eye. "You touch me and I'll rip your arm off and wrap it around your neck three times and stick your fingers up your nose."

Alex blinked and backpedaled his wheelchair. "Whatever you say, little lady. Besides, why should I bother with a guppy when I can have a rainbow trout." He winked in Debbie's direction. "Anytime you're ready to go fishing, let me know."

Ms. Cadena quickly stepped forward. "Why don't we just move on, here?"

Debbie leaned toward Barry and whispered, "Did he call me a fish?"

The horseman nodded. "Yeah. But it was a nice fish."

"That tall, good-lookin' fella over there beside Gina is David Jarboe from Seattle," Ms. Cadena announced.

The boy waved shyly. "I really like your farm . . . I mean, ranch," he said. "Is it OK if I do some shooting up in the mountains?"

Grandpa Hanson cleared his throat. "I'm sorry, David, but we don't allow hunting on my property. We believe that—"

"No, no," the teenager interrupted. "I don't mean with a gun." He reached into the van and pulled out a satchel. "I mean with a camera. I'm into photography. You know, pictures?"

The old man smiled broadly. "Of course, son. You can take all the pictures you want. Can't see how that'll get you into any trouble."

David grinned. "Well, that's not exactly true. I got arrested for taking a picture of Mrs. Thomlinson, my neighbor."

"What's so bad about that?" Joey wanted to know.

"She was . . . sorta . . . taking a bath at the time."

Wendy gasped. "How'd you do it? With a telephoto lens through the window or something?"

Mr. Hanson pressed his palm against his daughter's mouth. "Ah, David, would you mind not telling my youngest how you did what you did? She likes to experiment with new ideas."

Debbie joined in. "Right, unless you want to find yourself as an 8-by-10 hanging on her wall someday."

The boy smiled. "Sure thing. I'll keep my secrets to myself."

"But I want to know about the alligator," Wendy interjected.

David smiled. "That was all a terrible misunderstanding. Although it was kinda neat when my mom found him in our new jacuzzi—"

"And these are the two cousins I told you about," Ms. Cadena interrupted, making a proud sweep with her hand. "Lyle Burns and Judy Chisko. They're from Dallas, Texas, as you'll probably discover."

"Hi, y'all," Lyle called out, waving. "Cousin Judy is kinda shy. But she wants you to know how happy she is to be here."

The girl at his side nodded slightly, her bland expression looking like it was carved in stone.

"Matter of fact, I ain't seen her this worked up since that time her brother drove his car clean through their living room. He was kinda drunk at the time."

All eyes looked at Judy. One brow twitched.

"See what I mean?" Lyle gasped. "Even the mention of that night sets her off."

Samantha walked up to the girl and stared at her. "Is your face broken?" she asked.

"Samantha!" Lizzy called.

The little girl reached up and took Judy's hand

in her own. "You want to see the spider I caught this morning? It's really pretty. Has long legs and yellow spots all over it."

Judy nodded and followed this new friend in the direction of the horse barn. Lyle spread his hands. "Have you ever seen such absolute glee in one person before? I just know Cousin Judy's gonna love this ranch."

The silent teen and the little girl strolled down the path and headed over the footbridge as Ms. Cadena continued her introductions, giving the names of each of the Station inhabitants. Once everyone knew who everyone else was, the job of unloading the van began in earnest. There were rooms to be assigned and suitcases to unpack. Now that the new guests had arrived, summer at Shadow Creek Ranch could officially begin.

All during the process, Wrangler Barry kept a sharp eye on the boy in the wheelchair. He figured if he could keep Debbie safe from a Montana blizzard he could certainly save her from the clutches of this two-wheeled romeo. Or die trying.

CHAPTER 3

Master of the Morning

🦅 🦅 🦅

Somewhere, far away, water was dripping. It wasn't a quick or steady sound, the kind a leaky faucet makes. Rather, a soft *splat . . . splat.* The sound reverberated along dark corridors and reached the ears of the waking girl only occasionally, randomly, as if time had stolen the urgency from the noise and left it to disturb the silence at its own pace.

Dark eyes fluttered open and stared into the half-light of dawn. What was this place? What were those sounds?

Plenty sat up quickly, her breathing stopped, her mouth open.

Then she remembered. Red Stone. The mountains. The cave.

Even though it had been a few days since she and her great-grandfather left the comfortable, secure surroundings of their prairie reservation, the girl hadn't quite adjusted to waking up somewhere other than in her cozy bed. Sleeping on a pile of pine needles was going to take some getting used to.

She looked about the shadowed chamber. Embers from last night's fire still glowed beneath the large, cast-iron pot that hung from a metal frame by the far wall. Rough, wooden chairs rested beside the small stack of suitcases she and her white-haired companion had brought with them. Other than a few containers stuffed with food, and several plastic milk jugs filled with water fetched from a nearby stream, the cave was empty.

Plenty lay back down on her blanket and closed her eyes. She thought of her father, tall and handsome, walking out to his battered pickup truck in the early morning light as he did day after day, year after year. Mother would leave soon thereafter, heading for her parttime job as clerk in Pryor's only business establishment—a small grocery store a few doors from their mobile home. The woman would always pause and gaze at the mountains rising to the west, then continue on her way.

It was a morning ritual the young Indian girl had witnessed for as long as she could remember— her father heading for the coal fields, and her mother walking to the grocery store down the dusty street.

But Plenty had thoughts of neither coal fields nor mountains. Her mind continually wandered across the table-flat lands to the east, where the winds rustled the grasses and whispered words only she could hear.

"Come, Plenty." A familiar voice shattered her reverie. "It's time. Hurry, or you'll miss it."

The girl sighed and tried to ignore the invitation.

"Come quickly," the voice called again. "It's going to be more beautiful than yesterday."

Plenty rose on one elbow and looked toward the mouth of the cave where Red Stone sat, wrapped in a blanket, gazing intently out across the mountaintops.

"I've seen it before," the girl said.

"Oh, but it's always different, always new," Red Stone encouraged. "A Crow warrior must greet the sun or the day will turn against him."

Plenty shook her head. "I'm not a warrior, Great-grandfather. And neither are you."

Even as she spoke those last words she knew they'd hurt the old man at the cave entrance. Quickly she added, "Because we're not on the reservation. Indians are warriors only when they watch the sun rise over their own land."

"But this *is* my land," the old man retorted. "The people at Shadow Creek Ranch gave it to me."

"It was not theirs to give!" Plenty shot back, her words angry. "How can a man offer something to someone else if it's not his to begin with?"

"Just come," Red Stone insisted. "It'll happen any moment now. You must see it. You must greet the sun when it rises. It's the duty of every warrior."

Plenty sighed and tossed back her thin blanket. "OK, Great-grandfather," she moaned. "I will watch the sunrise with you, if it'll make you happy."

"Good," Red Stone smiled. "It's good that you do it."

The young girl shuffled to the entrance of the cave and sat down heavily beside the old man. She glanced to the east, where the mountains rolled like an angry sea in the soft, gray light of dawn.

Mt. Blackmore stood somber and silent, its summit still wearing the white, winter cap left by the storms that had raged across the region not many months before.

"There," Red Stone whispered. "Do you see it?"

Plenty nodded slowly. "Yes, Great-grandfather. I see it."

At first it was a tiny flicker, like a candle glowing far, far away. Then it spread, becoming a ball of flame, casting long, straight shafts of light high into the sky, piercing the shadows, brushing the mountaintops with yellow and gold hues.

The trees seemed to burst into smokeless flame as the brilliant circle of the sun continued to rise above the eastern lip of the land. Higher and higher the glowing sphere ascended until all reminders of night had vanished, leaving the mountain ranges, forest, and meadows bathed in the pure, radiant glare of a new day.

Red Stone stood to his feet and lifted his hands, his arms spread apart like an eagle in flight. "Master of the Morning!" he called out in words gathered from the ancient, timeless vocabulary of the Crow nation. "I greet you. I welcome you. Guide my steps during your journey across the sky. Bless my day with understanding. And may my heart be filled with compassion for all who walk in your light."

Golden rays pierced the cave entrance and touched every rock, every stone, with a glow no man-made invention could duplicate. The old Indian remained standing, letting the warmth of the light caress his face as it had for decades past.

Ever since he was a little boy running to keep up with his father through these very mountains, and spending the summer months in this very cave, he'd felt the warmth of the rising sun on his face. It was here he'd first heard the mournful cry of a hawk, the bark of a coyote, the snarl of a mountain lion. Right here, at the entrance to this cave, he'd watched his father stand and greet the morning, using the solemn, sacred words he'd just repeated.

But now there were no warriors left to welcome the rising sun—only men with jobs to drive to, mortgages to pay, duties to perform. When daylight broke across the land, no one took notice, and the Master of the Morning had to arrive unwelcomed, unheralded, unannounced.

Red Stone let his gaze fall to the forests below. The tradition would end with him. There was no one to take his place. No one, except Plenty.

* * *

"What's this stuff supposed to be?" Alex wrinkled his nose and pushed his spoon through the steaming mound in his breakfast bowl.

Grandma Hanson chuckled as she passed a jar of honey to the teenager sitting beside her. "It's bear mush," she announced.

"Bear what?" Alex exclaimed, dropping his utensil and backing away from the table.

"Bear mush. Haven't you ever heard of it in San Francisco?"

The boy shook his head. "We don't eat bears in California."

Wendy ladled a thick layer of honey over her liberal helping of the morning fare. "It's made from ground-up grizzly," she announced. "Claws and all. Here, honey helps cover the taste."

The boy's eyes opened wider. "I'm not eating a bear, no matter how much honey you dump on it."

Joey burst out laughing. "It's not made out of bear meat. We're all vegetarians on Shadow Creek Ranch."

Grandma Hanson grinned. "I'm sorry. I didn't mean to startle you with that rather unusual name. It's just made out of wheat. Why it's called bear mush I haven't a clue."

Alex relaxed a little. "Are there any more strange names I should know about before I get started?"

Debbie shook her head. "Nope. That's milk, that's peach jam, those are blueberry muffins, Gina's got the butter, and those sausages over there are made from soy beans."

The boy smiled and lifted a muffin and inspected it carefully. "I was thinkin', Debbie. How 'bout you and me goin' on a picnic today? Just the two of us. We could get—shall we say—better acquainted?"

Debbie picked up her spoon and blew softly on its steaming contents. "I've got an even better idea, Alex," she said.

The boy looked first one way, then another. Leaning forward, he spoke invitingly. "And what would that be?"

"Why don't we all take our first riding lesson? There's a horse out in the pasture who'd love to show you the sights."

The boy frowned. "And just how am I supposed to ride a horse? I'm in a wheelchair, if you haven't noticed."

"You'll see," Debbie smiled sweetly.

"*I* want to learn how to ride," David interjected from the far end of the food-laden table. "The only time I was ever on a horse was at a county fair. I was just 9 years old and this guy led us around for about 10 minutes. Wasn't very exciting."

Joey swallowed a glass of milk and wiped the white mustache it left above his lip with the back of his sleeve. "No one's gonna lead you around here," he said firmly. "These ain't kiddie horses. They're the real thing."

"Great!" David grinned excitedly. "May I bring my camera?"

"Sure," the young wrangler nodded. "You can stick it in your saddle bag and take it with you wherever you go."

Mr. Hanson cleared his throat. "Ah . . . David. That big box we received before you came. Is everything in it OK?"

"Yup."

The man nodded. "Nothing was . . . ah . . . broken . . . or wrinkled . . . or cracked?"

"Nope. Everything was just fine, thank you."

Wendy lifted her finger. "Wouldn't want anything bad to happen to . . . whatever's inside."

David smiled. "I appreciate that."

The girl paused. "Do you need any help unloading . . . or assembling . . . or painting . . . or arranging what's inside?"

David chuckled, enjoying the mystery his box seemed to have created in the minds of his new friends. "What I really need is a room, a room with no windows in it. But it has to have electricity. Is that possible?"

Grandpa Hanson scratched his head. "You want a room with no windows?"

"Yeah. And close to a bathroom."

Lizzy blinked. "A bathroom?"

"If it's not too much trouble."

Grandpa Hanson shrugged. "Well, we do have a storeroom at the end of the hall. Bathroom's just next door. Will that be OK?"

"Perfect!" David grinned. "Joey, could you help me put my box in that storeroom right after breakfast?"

The young horseman nodded slowly. "Sure thing, . . . David."

With that piece of business taken care of, the excited group hungrily devoured the delicious meal Grandma Hanson and Lizzy had prepared. Occasionally, Wendy would glance in David's direction and stop chewing. Then she'd shake her head and continue with her breakfast. Whatever was in the box would have to remain a mystery for a little while longer, as painful as the wait might be.

When all had cleaned their plates, Mr. Hanson stood to his feet. "Attention, everyone," he said with a smile. "I'd like to talk to you for a few moments." Voices stilled into attentive silence.

"This is the very first full day of your visit. I just want you to know how happy we are that you've agreed to spend a few weeks with us out here on the ranch.

"You're probably wondering why we do this sorta thing—working with Project Youth Revival, and all. The answer is simple. My father and I, along with my mother and Lizzy Pierce, firmly believe that this world has far too much sadness, violence, and hate in it. Crowded cities and drug-filled streets tend to support those unpleasant facts.

"But here on Shadow Creek Ranch we've dedicated our summers to showing teens like you that the world can be a pleasant place, a safe place. We're Christians. We believe in a God who says we should love our neighbors, and do unto others as we want them to do to us.

"The most important lesson we want you to learn during the next six weeks is that it *is* possible to live without hatred, without violence and fear, and that any sadness you may carry in your heart can be shared, and we won't laugh or make fun. Do you understand?"

Heads around the table nodded slowly.

"We're not perfect. We make mistakes. But we're

trying to help you as best we can. So, Gina, Alex, David, Lyle, and Judy, welcome to Montana, and welcome to Shadow Creek Ranch."

A cheer rose from those gathered about the table as chairs slid back and happy voices ushered in the new day. With excitement building, the group rushed out of the Station and headed for the pasture, where the ranch's small herd of horses waited by the corral.

Joey and David carefully carried Alex and his wheelchair down the porch steps and the three hurried in the direction of the footbridge.

"How am I going to ride a horse?" the handicapped boy kept saying over and over again. "I'll probably fall off the dumb animal and paralyze the rest of me."

Lizzy shook her head and smiled as she watched the happy procession from her kitchen window. Then, as she was turning around to attack the piles of breakfast dishes waiting by the sink, she jumped. Gina was standing in the doorway.

"Oh, you startled me! I thought everyone was heading for the corral."

The girl smiled shyly. "I'm not all that interested in horses," she said. "Is that OK?"

"Sure. We learned that lesson last summer." Lizzy lowered a wobbly tower of bowls into the suds. "Had a boy who spent most of his time glued in front of Mr. Hanson's computers."

"I'm not into computers much, either," the youngster admitted. "But I do like trains, you know, steam locomotives, coal cars, stuff like that."

Lizzy nodded. "I've ridden on a few choo-choos. And that was before they were considered a novelty in this country."

"You did?" Gina stepped to the sink and thrust her hands into the soap bubbles, searching for a dishrag. "I've only ridden on one steam train, down in Pennsylvania. It didn't go very far. But the sound and the power was really somethin'. I loved the smoke and embers blowing past the window and the rattle of those big iron wheels. It was really neat."

Lizzy took in a deep breath and gazed out the window as if searching for some long-forgotten memory. "I'd go to upstate New York with my aunt every summer. I was just a kid—5, 6 years old. But I remember the hissing, belching steam engine that pulled the cars. To tell you the truth, it scared me to death. I'd close my eyes until we were safe in our seats and the doors had been locked."

Gina sighed. "I wish I was born a long time ago like you." Her words softened. "Then maybe I could be someone else."

"Is there anything in particular wrong with being Gina McClintock?"

"Well, to begin with, that's not my real name."

"It isn't?"

The girl shook her head. "I'm adopted. Mr. and Mrs. McClintock raised me since I was a baby."

Lizzy tilted her head slightly. "Don't you mean 'Mom and Dad' raised you?"

"I used to call them that," the girl sighed. "Not anymore. They've changed."

"How?"

"Well, for starters, they treat me differently. They're always making up rules that I'm supposed to follow, you know. Like, when I'm supposed to come in at night, who I can and can't see, the clothes I can wear, the kind of music I should listen to. I don't have any freedom. They treat me like a little baby." The teenager wiped strands of brown hair from her forehead with the back of her hand. "I don't like it."

Lizzy nodded slowly as she carefully dried a serving bowl and lifted it into the cupboard. "Growing up's not easy. Take it from me, a young person needs all the help he or she can get. Maybe your adoptive parents are just trying to keep you safe, trying to keep you from making painful mistakes."

The girl's upper lip tightened. "Well, I don't see it that way. They just bug me. I hate them."

"Gina. You can't mean that. It seems to me like they want what's best for you."

The girl turned sharply. "You sound just like they do. They're always saying, 'We're only doing what's best for you. We're only doing what's best for you.' They're ruining my life! That's what they're doing. My birth mother wouldn't be like that. She'd be kind and loving. She'd be my friend. She'd understand what it's like to be me, because I'm part of her."

Sudden tears spilled down the girl's flushed cheeks. "And you don't understand, either. You're the same as they are!"

Gina threw the wet dishrag into the pile of suds, sending soapy water cascading against the window and open cupboards. "I came out here only to get away from my parents." She stormed to the doorway and stopped, her back to Lizzy. "I know what I have to do. And no one can stop me."

Lizzy watched the girl rush from the room and listened as her footsteps echoed through the lobby and out onto the porch. The front door slammed shut, leaving the old woman standing, dish in hand, alone in the kitchen.

Mr. Hanson appeared on the upper balcony. "Mrs. Pierce? Is everything all right?"

Lizzy walked out of the kitchen and stood at the base of the stairs. "I'm afraid not," the woman said softly. "We've got a problem with Gina. I've seen that kind of rage before." She turned and looked up at her friend. "In Joey."

Mr. Hanson lifted his eyebrows. "What're we going to do?"

"I'm not sure, Tyler. I need to talk with Ms. Cadena about this. Is she coming out today?"

"At 3:00."

Lizzy nodded. "Good."

With that she turned and headed for the kitchen. There were dishes to wash, and plans to make.

* * *

Alex looked down from his lofty perch and frowned. It seemed to him that he was at least 20 feet in the air when, in reality, the horse's back wasn't more than five and a half feet above the ground.

Joey rubbed his chin and nodded slowly. "I think it'll work."

"You *think*?" Alex gasped. "No, no. That's not good. You gotta *know* this contraption that you and Montana Slim over there threw together is going to keep me from killing myself. It's my rear end on the line here."

Joey chuckled. "My partner's name is Barry Gordon. He's the head wrangler. I'm his assistant."

"Forget the politics. Just guarantee me that this . . . this . . . gizmo whatchacallit is gonna save my hide when Rover here decides to gallop into the sunset with me strapped to his backbone."

The young wrangler laughed again. "Your horse's name isn't Rover. It's Lightning."

Alex's face paled. "You've got me bolted onto a horse named Lightning? Listen, I changed my mind. Get me down from here and I'll never do another bad thing as long as I live. I'll become a monk, a missionary, a preacher! Just don't let me die in Montana on a horse named after a destructive discharge of static electricity."

Wrangler Barry limped over and stood beside the animal. "What's the problem here?" he asked, throwing a quick wink in Joey's direction.

"So you're the head honcho around here," Alex said, his hands tightly gripping the oversized saddle horn. "How come you weren't at breakfast? I thought everyone ate together in this outfit."

"Didn't have time," Barry announced. "Was too

busy building the gizmo whatchacallit you're sitting on."

Alex glanced at Joey. "Whatta guy. Gave up his bear mush so I could die on a dumb animal called Lightning."

Joey shook his head. "You're not gonna die. Barry and I just made some adjustments so you won't slip, that's all. Most riders use their legs for balance and to keep themselves from falling off the back of their horses."

"But since my legs are useless," Alex interrupted, "you had to make this stupid glorified infant seat for me." The boy sighed. "I suppose you think I should be thankful."

"Don't strain yourself," Barry said coldly. "Wouldn't want to see you left behind when everyone heads for the sunset." The wrangler turned, then paused. "Lightning's a good horse. He'll watch out for you." Barry stabbed the ground with his cane. "And stop complaining. At least you can ride."

"Hey," Alex called. "Like you can't? I don't see you stuck in a wheelchair."

The wrangler lifted his chin as if to respond, then hobbled toward the corral.

"Take it easy, Alex," Joey whispered. "Barry *can't* ride. The bouncing hurts his guts too much. He had an accident last winter and he ain't healed yet. So don't go messin' with him, OK?"

Alex watched the young man with the cane move carefully through the entrance to the horse barn.

"He can work some," Joey continued. "He can do stuff at the bench with his hands, but he can't ride, pitch hay, or even saddle the horses." The speaker's eyes narrowed. "He's my best friend, anyway. So just don't mess with him, you understand me?"

Alex nodded. "Whatever you say, cowboy. You're in charge. But don't try to make me feel sorry for Roy Rogers over there. I've got problems of my own."

Joey shook his head and was about to offer a response using a few choice words he'd learned on the streets of New York when he remembered a phrase Lizzy Pierce often repeated. "Silence is the best defense." Even Grandpa Hanson had read a verse in the Bible that said something about a soft answer turning away wrath. So Joey held his tongue and smiled up at the boy through gritted teeth. "Looks like the others are about ready to go. We'd better join them." He spoke with as much enthusiasm as he could muster.

"Why not?" Alex muttered. "At least I'll have a chance to bug ol' Debbie some more. I think she likes me but is just too shy to admit it."

Joey hid a grin as he led Lightning toward the cottonwoods, where the others waited. Debbie? Shy? Yeah, right.

* * *

The morning went well, considering that Lyle and Judy kept getting their horses tangled up with each other, David rode under a tree and emerged with a mouthful of leaves, Gina could never keep her feet in the stirrups, and Alex kept telling Debbie how wonderful she looked with her long, dark hair tied up in a pony tail.

Joey suggested to Alex that maybe he should concentrate a little more on learning to ride his horse.

Debbie said she was flattered but, no, she didn't want to run off to Las Vegas with him just yet.

Wendy told him to shut up.

But by lunch time, each of the new arrivals had grown accustomed to the somewhat unpredictable movements horses make as they trot through meadows and along forest trails. The group traveled in a big circle around the valley, always within a short distance of the Station. The route had been carefully designed to challenge the new riders, yet allow them ample space to learn the most effective ways of informing their horses what direction to go and how fast to get there.

At noon, sack lunches were delivered to a pre-selected meadow by Grandpa Hanson, and the group gathered in the shade of a tall hardwood to enjoy the delicious meal Grandma Hanson and Lizzy had prepared.

"Do you know what I think?" David called out, moving his words around a mouthful of wheat bread piled with lettuce and tomatoes.

Lyle, savoring the flavor of an enormous red apple, sighed a contented sigh. "I think we're all about to find out," he teased good-naturedly.

David grinned. "Someday, I'm going to move to

Montana and open a photo shop in a little town and take pictures for *National Geographic*."

Joey raised his eyebrows. "Sounds like a great idea. You could specialize in photographing horses for ranchers. I'd even hire you to take a picture of Tar Boy, after I cleaned him up a bit." He admired the large, black animal grazing with the other horses nearby.

Alex shook his head. "You wanna show me how you can tell a clean horse from a dirty horse? They all look the same to me."

Wendy chuckled as she carefully folded a sandwich wrapper and returned it to her sack. "Tar Boy's always dirty. Early's always clean. That's how you can tell."

"Well, I think that's a wonderful idea," Debbie said with a smile. "David could open his shop up in Deer Lodge, or somewhere near Flathead Lake. Lots of tourists head that direction in the summer." She turned. "How 'bout you, Gina? What're you going to do after you finish high school?"

The girl shrugged. "I'm gonna be rich. I won't have to work."

"You are?" Debbie asked. "Do your folks have lots of money?"

Gina tossed her half-eaten sandwich back into her bag. "The McClintocks?" She laughed. "I'm not going to be like them. They're always working and saving and making big plans about how they're going to send me to some stupid college and buy me a stupid computer and all. Well, they won't have to bother. They can keep their nickels and dimes. I'm going to be so rich I can do whatever I please."

Debbie grinned. "You got an uncle who owns a gold mine or something?"

The girl with the rosy cheeks and blue eyes brushed bread crumbs from her lap. "Yeah, somethin' like that."

"Cousin Judy's grandfather had a gold mine once," Lyle announced with a big, Texas grin, his words heavily edged with a southern drawl. "Made more money than he knew what to do with. Then he died. Went to bed one night and didn't wake up. Butler found him the next morning stiff as a board."

"Really?" Wendy gasped, leaning forward. "An honest-to-goodness gold mine? Where is it?"

"That's the problem," Lyle continued. "He never told anyone where it was. The families have been searching for years, and all anybody comes up with are rattlesnakes and sagebrush. Ain't that right, Cousin Judy?"

The girl sitting beside him moved her head in what looked like a gesture of agreement. "See how distraught my cousin is?" Lyle shook his head sadly. "It's something we don't talk about too often. Shakes her up pretty bad, as you can see."

Wendy and the others stared at the silent, unmoving girl.

"Don't worry," Lyle encouraged with a smile. "She'll get it out of her system soon enough. We'll just have to be patient, that's all."

After a few moments, the girl lifted her hand to her mouth and took a bite of her sandwich. "There," Lyle announced, "the worst is over."

Wendy blinked. "Your cousin is a very interesting person."

"Isn't she, though?" the boy agreed. "She's always been a real inspiration to me and my whole family."

Joey glanced at Wendy, then at Debbie. "Well, enough chatter. Let's get back on our horses and continue our riding lessons. David and Lyle, you wanna help me get ol' Alex back up on Lightning?"

Lunch sacks were quickly collected and stowed in worn saddle bags. Before long, the meadow stood empty except for a small pile of bread crumbs left for the furry creatures that Joey, Wendy, and Debbie knew were waiting at the edge of the forest.

Unseen by the departing riders, several bushes trembled at the far end of the meadow and a shadowy form moved silently behind the tree line. The picnickers, every movement had been watched, their words overheard, their laughter noticed by a young, unseen visitor. A crow called overhead, then flapped away, its wings dark against the blue, cloudless sky.

CHAPTER 4

First Prisoner

♦ ♦ ♦

Evening shadows lengthened across the folds of the mountain range as Plenty sat gazing at the valley far below. From her vantage point, she could see all of Shadow Creek Ranch—the Station, horse barn, tack house, pasture, and the silvery creek that wound through it like a weaver's thread.

The air was chill, as it always was this high in the Gallatins. To her back, beyond the meadow where the grasses swayed in the evening breezes, stood Mount Blackmore, eternal snows softening its jagged summit. Up range and much closer waited Freedom Mountain, its crest too low to wear winter's coat during summer months.

Plenty sighed and let her gaze settle on the distant way station. Everyone had gone inside about an hour ago. She'd seen them, moving slowly along the driveway. Her eyes, accustomed to the vast spaces of the prairie, had become very adept at seeing details from far away. Red Stone had often commented on the sharpness of her eyesight. "A warrior needs clear vision," the old man would say proudly.

Warrior. The word seemed to taste bad in Plenty's mouth whenever she spoke it. It didn't describe her, that was for sure. She was just a young girl who spent her days on the Crow Indian reservation in south-central Montana.

A warrior would never live as she did. He'd be free, free to pitch his tent where he chose. Free to run across the flatlands, to move silently in the night, to hunt where no barbed-wire fences divided the pastures, where no White-man buildings stood, where no logging roads felt the rumble of trucks, where no chain saws shaved away the forests, leaving the land naked, scarred.

No, she wasn't a warrior. Never could be. The past had stripped her people of such noble beings, leaving behind mere shadows of the men and women who used to roam this land, who used to splash in mountain streams and fall in love under unpolluted skies.

Her once-proud Crow nation, survivors of blizzards, droughts, and prairie fires, had fallen victim to the worst kind of disaster—the encroachment of White people from the east, across tribal lands, across sacred mountains, across dreams.

The sun slipped below the horizon, leaving behind a golden glow that slowly faded until night stars blinked to life across the vast canopy of sky. Plenty turned and faced Freedom Mountain. She lingered for just a moment, studying the dark outline beyond the meadow. "All the warriors are gone, Great-grandfather," she whispered, knowing no one heard. "They're all gone."

With a sigh, the girl began to walk along the path she knew would lead her directly to the cave. It was a path Red Stone had worn through the years as he'd come to sit alone, gazing down at the valley where his memories lived, where he'd spent summer days with his father.

A deep sadness crept into the teenager's heart, a feeling as cold as the air she breathed. Why did she have to be born an Indian? Why did she have to live with a past filled with such pain, such heartache?

She melted into the shadows as, far below, lights glowed from the Station windows.

* * *

Five tired, dirt-stained but happy teenagers slumped into the high-ceilinged den and collapsed at selected spots around the cozy room. China and silver clanked down the hall as Grandma Hanson and Lizzy waged war with the piles of dirty dishes.

The women smiled at each other, knowing this would be the last night they'd have to attack the job alone. Starting tomorrow morning, two of the five visitors would be assigned as their helpers for the summer. The adults had decided that, for the first full day of their visit, the new arrivals could just play.

"I think my legs are going to fall off," David moaned, rubbing his thighs. "Do you have any narrower horses I can ride?"

Joey laughed. "You'll get use to it."

Lyle shook his head. "Judy and I are beat." Everyone glanced at the girl who sat bolt upright in her chair by the window. "Just look at her," Lyle continued. "She's really done in. Don't be too surprised if she's not her usual, bubbly self this evening."

Wendy blinked. "Oh, we won't."

"Comin' through!" Alex burst into the room, his wheelchair sending Samantha and Mr. Hanson scattering for safety. "Man, I ate like a pig," the boy announced. He stopped in the middle of the room and spun his chair around and around on its large main wheels. "Those two women sure know how to whip up a tasty pile of chow."

Mr. Hanson chuckled. "I'll be sure that the women hear of your kind compliment."

Alex nodded. "Hey, your honor. How's the lawyering business? Hung any bad guys today?"

The man paused for just a moment. "Not yet," he said.

Gina pressed her face against the window glass and gazed out across the front lawn. "Sure gets dark around here."

Samantha tilted her head to one side. "Don't you have night where you come from?"

Joey laughed and grabbed his sister, smothering her with hugs. "Of course, she has night," he said. "But in the city, there're so many lights, it's hard to tell. Don't you remember what it was like in New York?"

The little girl shrugged. "I don't remember New

York anymore. I only remember Shadow Creek Ranch."

"Good," the boy responded. "I wish I could do that."

Grandpa Hanson strode into the room and took his place by the hearth. "I see everyone survived their first day with us. Hope you all had a good time."

Heads nodded enthusiastically around the room.

"Terrific. Tomorrow, we get down to the business of running a ranch. Each of you will be given a main task to perform while you're guests here. I've studied you carefully during our short time together and have assigned you work based on what I think you'll get the most benefit from.

"We'll begin with Gina. I noticed at supper that you were quite taken by the vegetarian dishes we served. You said you were amazed that meatless foods could taste so good. That's why I'm assigning you as assistant cook. You'll be working with Mrs. Pierce in the kitchen for one meal a day."

Gina lifted her hand to protest, then lowered it. Of all the jobs she imagined a ranch to contain, this one might be the least offensive. At least she wouldn't be shoveling horse manure out in the corral.

"I talked to David earlier and he showed me some of the pictures he'd taken in the Seattle area—the ones where people were fully clothed," the old man continued with a grin. "They're very good. So, Mr. Jarboe, I'm making you the official photographer of the group. Your job is to create a scrapbook for each of us to enjoy in the coming years—sort of a report, if you know what I mean. Ms. Cadena says she could always use pictures of Project Youth Revival in action. I understand that your box will come in handy for this purpose."

Wendy looked up sharply. "Box? Did you say box?" She glanced over at David. "I can help. I'll be your assistant. We can begin by unpacking that box, OK?"

David chuckled. "Thanks, Grandpa Hanson. I'd like that. 'Cept I don't have much film. It's kinda expensive."

Tyler Hanson cleared his throat. "I've opened an account for you at the photo store in Bozeman. You can get what you need there."

"Wow!" David enthused. "You mean anything?"

"Within reason," the young lawyer grinned. "Let's keep in mind that we have to eat around here."

David sat back in his chair, an excited smile creasing his slightly sunburned face. "I'm going to try all the films I've read about in my magazines. Man! This is going to be my best summer ever!"

Grandpa Hanson nodded. "Good. Now, Alex." The boy spun his wheelchair around until he was facing the speaker. "I don't know nothin' about food or photography," he said. "But I'm great on dates. How 'bout assigning me as personal bodyguard and escort for Miss Debbie. I'll take good care of her. Really."

The old man chuckled. "That's not exactly what I had in mind. Joey tells me you handled yourself fairly well on Lightning today. He said you may be a natural horseman."

Alex looked at Grandpa Hanson sideways. "I don't

think I like where this conversation is leading."

"So," the man continued, "I'm assigning you as assistant wrangler for the summer."

"WHAT! You want me to take care of horses? I can't do that. I'm . . . I'm . . . handicapped, unless you haven't noticed."

"Oh, I've noticed," Grandpa Hanson said matter-of-factly. "I've also noticed that you're kinda pale around the cheeks. You need to be outdoors, in the fresh air, working those arm muscles instead of sit-tin' around watching baseball games on TV or"—he paused and looked the young man squarely in the eyes—"or using the phone to raise funds for nonex-istent charities."

Alex grinned. "You know about that, huh?"

"Yeah. So that's why we're going to teach you a new trade, out in the horse barn, where there are no phones. And you don't have to worry about TV either. Only get one station around here. PBS."

The teenager rolled his eyes. "Documentaries. I hate documentaries."

"Great, so it's settled. Report to Barry Gordon first thing tomorrow morning after breakfast."

Alex nodded with a frown. "Whatever you say."

"How 'bout Judy and me?" Lyle called. "Whatcha got planned for us?"

"Glad you asked," Grandpa Hanson smiled. "You two are going to help with the housework—you know, clothes washing, floor sweeping, trash collect-ing. Even with Joey and Wrangler Barry sleeping in the horse barn, that leaves 12 people living in the

Station. We need all the domestic help we can get."

"Say no more," Lyle beamed. "Cousin Judy and I will gladly lend a hand to the daily chores of this fine establishment. We'd be honored to keep everything in tip-top condition, right, Cousin Judy?" The girl lowered her head slightly. "She's as honored as I am," Lyle announced.

"Fantastic," Grandpa Hanson responded enthusiastically. "Now everyone has a job to do. Your duties won't take but an hour and a half a day, at the most. We'll also have two of you help with the dishes every meal. I'll post a schedule so you'll know when it's your turn. After your chores are done, you're free to enjoy whatever the ranch has to offer."

Alex yawned. "Right now the only thing I'd like to enjoy is my bed. Any objections?"

"Sounds good to me," Joey replied, rising. "Wrangler Barry's probably snoring already. Guess I'll join him. We make a great duet."

David glanced over at Wendy. "Hey, partner," he said. "We'll open the box first thing tomorrow, OK?"

"OK!" Wendy smiled. "Right after breakfast. And there'd better not be an alligator in there."

"You'll have to wait and see," David teased.

One by one, sleepy people stumbled from the room, calling goodnights to each other. Soon the Station settled into silence as a full moon looked down from above, washing the valley with soft, silver light.

* * *

Rumble . . . rumble . . . CRASH! Thunder shook

the Station as dawn arrived cold and gray. Rain fell heavily from dark, rolling clouds, obscuring the mountains and filling the creek bed with muddy torrents of water.

Wrangler Barry stirred, awakened from a dream about a time long past when he was a little boy. He was searching for his pony, Trotter. He couldn't find him anywhere. He kept calling his name over and over until the thunder snatched sleep from his mind.

The young man pushed himself up on one elbow and stared into the dimly lit workshop. Saddles hung neatly on low beams of wood. Colorful blankets moved in the occasional gust that whistled through the long, narrow boards forming the back wall of the corral.

He was startled to see Joey sitting on his cot by the workbench, staring at him.

"Hey, Joey." The wrangler greeted his friend with a not-quite-awake grin. "What're you doin' up so early?"

"Who's Trotter?" his young companion asked from across the room.

Barry chuckled. "Sometimes I dream too loudly."

Another bolt of lightning lit the cracks in the wall. This was followed quickly by a window-rattling thump of thunder.

"He was my first pony," the older wrangler yawned. "Brown. Speckled. Loved to eat my mom's roses."

"Bet she appreciated that," Joey grinned.

"Oh, yeah. They were best of pals."

Wrangler Barry stretched his good arm and

began massaging his other. This was something he had to do each day to get the injured limb to operate with any degree of success.

"Did they tell him?"

Joey nodded. "Yup."

"How'd he take it?"

The younger boy shrugged. "How do you think?"

Barry grimaced as he rose slowly to his feet. "There's something about Alex that bothers me. Not just his big mouth or his high regard for himself. It's . . . how he says what he says. His attitude."

Joey stretched and yawned. "I used to know guys like him in New York."

"What'd you do about it?"

"Beat the tar out of 'em. 'Course, that was the old Joey Dugan."

Barry collected his cane and shuffled across the room and sat down on a bundle of straw. "I know what it's like to . . . to not be able to do things."

Joey nodded.

"I figured if anybody here could help him, I could. 'Cept I don't have a clue how to go about it. I haven't exactly worked things out myself."

The younger wrangler lay back on his bunk. "Dizzy used to tell me it took a whole lot less energy to be kind than to be nasty. I used to work very hard at being nasty. She's right. Wears you out."

Barry smiled. "Strange. I can't picture you as a street punk." The horseman paused. "What made the change?"

Joey thought for a long moment. "Someone

believed in me when I didn't believe in myself."

"You mean Mr. Hanson?"

"Yeah. And Grandpa Hanson. Dizzy." Joey glanced at his companion. "And you."

Barry nodded slowly. It seemed so simple. Show someone you have faith in them, and they'll change. Right? But what if you don't have enough faith in yourself? What if the very person you're trying to help carries the same hurt in his heart as you do? It would be like the blind leading the blind. Or in this case, the cripple leading the cripple.

THUMP. An object slammed against the corral door, making Joey and Barry jump. "What was that?" the boy on the cot called.

The wrangler hobbled to the wide doorway. "It sounded like something hit the corral."

Joey hurried over and lifted the metal latch. Rain stung his face as he eased open the door and peered into the dim light of dawn. He could see nothing.

Lightning flashed, freezing the raindrops in midair like a camera captures an image. In the sudden light he thought he saw a figure running along the line of cottonwoods, but he wasn't sure.

Turning to close the door, he gasped. "Barry! Look at this!"

The wrangler stumbled out into the downpour and stood gazing at the boards that formed the entrance to the horse barn. There, embedded in the stout, rough-hewn wood, was a handmade arrow. Joey reached up and worked the shaft free, then rushed back into the barn, Barry limping at his heels.

The two stood staring at the carefully crafted object, neither speaking. When Joey found words, they were spoken with a quiet fear. "I think we have a problem here," he said. "A big, big problem."

* * *

Mr. Hanson rubbed his unshaved chin and slowly turned the arrow over and over in his hands. It was a work of art; finely chiseled stone point on one end and precisely positioned feathers fastened securely at the other end. Someone had taken great care in creating the deadly piece.

"You didn't see anyone at all?" the man repeated, his bathrobe hanging loosely over his shoulders.

Joey shook his head. "Just a movement at the tree line. Could've been a shadow. It wasn't light enough yet, and the storm was pretty intense."

The lawyer sighed. "We can't let the others know about this. It'll scare our guests half to death."

"Ain't exactly making me feel warm and fuzzy inside," Joey admitted. "I don't like having people shooting arrows at me. What if I'd opened the barn door at that very moment? Next Halloween I wouldn't have to buy one of those fake arrow-through-the-head gags. I'd have one for real."

Wrangler Barry tapped his cane on the floor. "Do you think it was one of the new arrivals playing a joke or something?"

"No way," Mr. Hanson said. "They wouldn't know how to construct such a beautiful piece as this, much less fire it with any degree of accuracy from the tree line. No, as far as I'm concerned, only someone who is a student of true Indian folklore would have the knowledge necessary to construct this arrow."

Joey looked at Barry, then at Mr. Hanson. "You're not thinking Red Stone, are you? He's our friend. You and your dad gave him a whole mountain last year. He wouldn't—" The speaker stopped mid-sentence as an unsettling thought gripped his mind.

Wrangler Barry, sensing the same conclusion, walked to the office window and gazed out across the rain-swept lawn and pasture. "Why would *she* do it?"

Mr. Hanson shrugged. "She's not exactly a fan of the White man. Sometimes the past pain of a tribe can surface among the young—violently. There've been many of what the newspapers call 'uprisings' on reservations during the past 100 years. People have died, Indian and White. This is no matter to be taken lightly."

Joey sat down heavily on the nearby office chair. "It's just like the streets. You do somethin' bad to me so I'm going to do somethin' bad to you."

"Revenge is nasty medicine," the lawyer responded. "I deal with it in almost every case I try. No one wins. Everyone loses."

"What're we going to do?" Barry asked, still watching the rain falling beyond the windowpane.

Joey stood. "Let me talk to Red Stone. I'm sure he doesn't even know what happened."

Mr. Hanson frowned. "Maybe we should just contact the leaders of her tribe at Crow Agency. They wouldn't want one of their own trying to take on the

White man single-handedly."

"Just let me try," Joey insisted. "I'll go up the mountain first thing after breakfast. It's too wet for riding lessons. Besides, maybe it was all just a practical joke."

Mr. Hanson studied the arrow lying across his hands. "You don't fire a deadly weapon as a joke, especially if you're an Indian."

Joey nodded. "Just let me talk to Red Stone, OK?"

The lawyer sighed a long sigh. "OK," he said quietly. "But Joey, be careful."

"Hey," the teenager responded with a determined grin. "I'm from East Village, remember?"

Mr. Hanson smiled. "I remember. Just watch your backside. I kinda like having you around. Don't ask me why."

Joey chuckled as he turned to leave. "As I've told you before, it's my shy, innocent nature. You can't help yourself."

"Your humility, too," the lawyer called after the disappearing horseman. "Just be careful."

"You got it," Joey's voice answered from the hallway.

Wrangler Barry shook his head. "I don't like this," he said.

Mr. Hanson tossed the arrow onto his desk and sighed. "What a way to start a summer."

* * *

Gina stood in the doorway of the kitchen, unsure of the welcome she'd receive. Her last visit had not gone well at all.

She looked about the spotlessly clean room and its brightly tiled floor. Carefully arranged pots and pans hung from a rectangular wooden frame suspended above a solidly built work island. A big four-burner range stood at one end of a long counter, sporting a copper heat vent like an oversized hat.

A huge refrigerator hummed quietly off to one side, keeping its store of food cold, ready for future meals.

Under the window rested the double sink, its white enamel worn down to metal in several places, testimony to the years of use it had sustained.

To her left, two microwave ovens sat side by side atop an old ice chest pushed up against the wall. Their modern, high-tech faces looked strangely out of place beside an even older dry sink that formed a serving platform for dishes headed for the dining room. An arched entryway separated the kitchen from the large eating area.

The kitchen had a look of efficiency and homeyness—a look the girl had admired the first time she'd seen it.

Several aprons hung from hooks on the pantry door. Gina ambled over to the closet-like alcove and studied the contents that burdened the thick shelves. Columns of canned goods wrapped in colorful pictures enticed the viewer to try what was inside. Cereal boxes stood tightly packed together on the next row while, just above, round, plastic containers offered abundant supplies of dried goods such as noodles and brown wheat flour.

The other wall sported well-braced shelves brimming with skillets, serving dishes, and canning jars.

The pantry was clean and orderly, just like the kitchen, just like the entire Station. These people were serious about their ranch, and their lives. Of this, Gina was sure. Seemed everything had a place, a purpose, a job to do.

"Hot cereal or omelettes?" a voice called from across the room. Gina turned to find Lizzy opening a cupboard and staring up at its contents.

"What?" Gina responded nervously.

"Should we make hot cereal or omelettes this morning?" the woman repeated.

Gina shrugged. "I like cheese omelettes. With hot sauce on them."

Lizzy nodded. "So do I. Sorta like Mexico meets France. Good choice."

Gina walked over to the sink and glanced out the window, not wanting to make eye contact with the woman. "Raining today," she said. "Can't go riding."

"Nope," Lizzy agreed, reaching for an apron and tossing it in the girl's direction. "There's only one word to describe a teenager who'd go horseback riding on a day like this."

"What's that?" Gina asked.

"Wet."

The girl blinked. "What?"

"Wet. You know. Un-dry?"

A grin played at the corners of Gina's mouth. "Yeah. Good word."

Lizzy fastened her own apron around her waist and brushed out its wrinkles. "So you want to learn how to cook vegetarian dishes, huh?"

"I guess so."

"The animals of the world thank you."

Gina's grin widened. "You think so?"

"Trust me," Lizzy called, heading into the pantry. "There are celebrations going on at slaughter houses around the world even as we speak." She emerged with a box of powdered milk in one hand, a mixing bowl in the other.

"Eggs are in the fridge. I'll fire up the burner. We don't fix eggs too much 'round here. Cholesterol, you know. But it's OK once in a while. Cheese, you say?"

"Yes. Lots of cheese."

"How 'bout just enough cheese to give the omelette flavor without clogging everyone's arteries? Deal?"

Gina nodded. "Deal."

Lizzy placed the ingredients on the work island. "Vegetarian, or health-conscious cooking, isn't just about not eating flesh foods. It's about being careful with whatever we put in our bodies. I guess it's possible to overdose on green beans or tossed salads. So, I'm going to teach you how to plan a balanced menu, how to bring out the natural taste of vegetables, and how to control the amount of sugar we dump down people's throats. Still interested?"

"Yes," Gina said enthusiastically. "I want to be healthy so I can—" She paused. "So I can have a good future."

"Noble cause," Lizzy agreed. "I've given Grandma Hanson the morning off so it'll be just you and me preparing breakfast, and lunch if you want." She motioned toward the refrigerator. "You get the eggs, I'll mix the milk. We'll have this breakfast on the table in no time flat."

Gina studied the energetic woman thoughtfully. Her real mother was probably just like that—funny, intense, caring. Maybe Shadow Creek Ranch wasn't going to be so bad, after all.

The girl pulled open the refrigerator door and began searching for the egg cartons. Maybe they'd even help her in her plan. But she'd better wait a little longer. Sometimes people aren't what they appear to be.

* * *

Thunder shook the ground as Joey guided Tar Boy along the narrow mountain trail. A steady rain beat the forest unmercifully, causing the leaves to quiver as if they too felt the uneasy fear the young horseman carried in his heart.

He'd faced troubles before. He couldn't count the number of times he'd walked down dark alleys and deserted city streets late at night, hurrying to meet a challenge thrown down by a rival gang member in East Village.

But this was different. He was going to have to face a young girl, an Indian no less, one who seemed to be very good with a bow and arrow.

He carried no weapon, except a small hunting

knife he always kept strapped to his belt. The knife was not for defense but for safety in the wilds. One never knew when it would be necessary to cut up a few small twigs for an emergency fire, or dig in the ground for life-sustaining roots, or try to deter a bobcat or other predator from attempting to turn you into a snack. He'd never had to use the knife in such an emergency, and as far as he was concerned, he wasn't about to begin using it now.

Tar Boy's big hooves slipped slightly in the mud as the two continued their journey along one of the few abandoned logging roads that led up Freedom Mountain. The rain increased, sending miniature waterfalls cascading over the lip of Joey's broad-rimmed hat and down the slick surface of his flapping raincoat.

"There it is," the boy whispered over the sound of the falling rain. "Do you see it, Tar Boy?"

The horse shook his head as if in response and lifted his young rider over the top of a small rise. At the crest of the mountain, beyond the dark-trunked forest, waited Red Stone's cave, its mouth yawning broadly through the deluge.

Joey stopped and studied the scene for a long moment. Nothing moved, except for the trees bending at the passage of each cold gust of wind.

Slowly, the boy dismounted and tied his horse's reigns loosely around a nearby bush.

He moved nervously toward the mouth of the grotto, glancing about for any signs of human life as he went.

Reaching the lip of the cave, he peered inside. He could see the blankets and cooking pot, the small collection of suitcases. Smoke rose from the hot ashes and half-burned wood of a still-flickering fire.

Joey stepped inside, listening, straining to hear any sound other than the wind-whipped rain falling behind him.

"Red Stone . . . Stone . . . Stone . . . Stone?" His call echoed and reechoed along unseen corridors in the darkness of the cave. "Hello . . . lo . . . lo . . . lo? Anybody here . . . ody here . . . ody here . . . ody here?"

There was no answer. Nothing moved in the shadows.

Joey turned and looked out into the rain. Tar Boy stood grazing on a collection of leaves, the long hairs of his mane wrinkled and clumped, his shoulders shining black and silver.

"No one's here, Tar Boy," Joey called from the cave entrance. "Must be out hunting or something."

He stepped forward. "Guess we may as well—"

Thump! An arrow sliced the air and struck deep into a tree trunk inches from the boy's head. Joey froze, watching the shaft vibrate, sending little sprays of water arching into the damp air.

"That's not funny," he called, motionless. "Someone could get hurt."

Thump! Another arrow pierced the bark just below the first.

"Stop it!" Joey demanded. "I mean it. This is stupid."

"Don't tell me the White man is scared?" a

88

young, female voice called from somewhere beyond the sheets of rain.

"I don't like being shot at," Joey countered. He waited for a response. There was none.

Slowly, he turned and faced the woods as rain drummed against his hat and coat. There was no movement among the bushes and low-lying branches.

"I don't want to fight you," he called. "Fighting only gets people hurt. It doesn't prove nothin'."

"I think it does," the unseen speaker responded, this time far to the right. Joey spun around. Squinting through the deluge, he could just make out the form of a girl standing atop a large rock about 50 feet away. In her grip, an arrow poised at full tension behind a straining, wooden bow.

Joey remained motionless. "Where's Red Stone?" he asked, trying not to let the form on the rock see his hands trembling.

"At the river," came the reply. "We saw you ride by. I knew you'd be coming. My great-grandfather is old and not very fast on his feet."

Joey shook his head. "Why don't you stop with the cowboy and Indian routine, Plenty? I just want to talk to you and Red Stone. That's all."

"What about?"

The boy laughed nervously. "What about? Well, let's see. The weather? Sports? The economy? Come on, Plenty. You're standing there with an arrow aimed at my head and you wonder what I want to talk to you about?"

Joey saw the girl lower the bow just a little, then raise it again. "You shouldn't be here. This is my great-grandfather's mountain."

"Well, you shouldn't shoot arrows into our barn, either. Why'd you do it? You got Mr. H all worked up. He's really worried. We've got guests down there, city kids. How'd it look if Project Youth Revival had to tell some juvenile delinquent's mother that her pride and joy is in the hospital because he was attacked by an Indian?"

Plenty shrugged. "The same things Indian moms were told after the White man raided villages and killed all their children."

"That was a long time ago!" Joey shouted, frustration forming his words. "We weren't even born yet. Our parents weren't even born, for goodness sake."

"Doesn't matter," the girl called through the rain. "I'm still Indian and you're still White. Nothing's changed. Nothing."

"Plenty?" An old man's voice called from down the path. "Plenty, is someone there with you?"

The girl turned. At that moment Joey let out a shrill whistle and started running in Tar Boy's direction. The big horse's head shot up, pulling the bush he was tied to clean out of the ground. With a bolt, the animal surged forward, running parallel with his master.

Before Plenty could reaim her arrow, she saw the young wrangler leap from a rock and arch through the air, landing hard on Tar Boy's broad back.

Joey's feet slammed into the stirrups as he bent low over the surging animal and, in an instant, both disappeared into the forest.

Red Stone entered the clearing and stopped to catch his breath. "Did I hear a horse?" he asked. "Did Joey come for a visit?"

Plenty lowered her bow and shook her head. "I was just target shooting," she said. "Maybe you heard my arrows hitting the tree. The horse and rider must've gone somewhere else after we saw them."

Red Stone shielded his eyes from the rain. At the mouth of the cave he could see two arrows jutting from the wet bark of a spruce.

"That must have been it," he said. "Sounded like horses' hooves. But in this rain, who can tell?" He continued walking up the path. "I was hoping young Dugan would pay us a visit. He's nice. Likes to hear my stories."

Plenty nodded and followed her great-grandfather to the mouth of the cave. Pausing by the tree, she carefully removed the arrows and returned them to the leather quiver strapped to her back.

She glanced in the direction Joey had headed and studied the quaking leaves through the blowing rain. He'd be back. The girl knew Joey Dugan was not the type to run away from a fight. They'd meet again. She just knew it.

* * *

Wendy stood beside the mysterious box as David eased a long table against the wall. Grandpa

Hanson had brought the table down from the attic for him. Stepping back, the boy gave a satisfied sigh.

"This is great," he said. "Should do fine."

His companion glanced about the windowless room with a degree of apprehension. "Why's it have to be so dark?" she asked. Then her eyes brightened and she leaned forward. "Do you work for the government?"

David laughed. "Hardly. They're always trying to lock me up."

"Oh, yeah," the girl nodded. "I forgot."

David rubbed his hands together. "Now, how 'bout we see what's in the box?"

Wendy stepped back just a little. "Don't let it bite me or I'll rip out its teeth."

"Don't worry," the boy chuckled. "What's inside doesn't have that many teeth."

With a yank David flipped open the top of the crate, revealing a sea of shredded newspapers. Confidently he thrust his hand through the pile and grabbed something underneath. Slowly, carefully, he lifted a long object into the light that spilled in from the open door.

Wendy saw two shiny parallel poles about three feet long and 12 inches apart. They were held together by a flat metal plate. A stubby handle jutted from the object; at the base of the poles she noticed a large, rectangular piece of wood.

"It's a launching pad for a rocket, right?" Wendy asked excitedly.

"Nope."

The boy buried his hands in the shredded newspaper again. This time they emerged with a round item that looked like it had accordion bellows built into it.

"It's a heart pump or a lung machine to help wounded soldiers on the battlefield!"

"Nope."

David fastened the bizarre object to the flat plate that straddled the parallel bars, leaving it suspended above the wooden base. Next he withdrew a small box from the shredded paper and opened it slowly. "This is the secret," he whispered. "This is what makes everything work." In his hand he held a small, metal cylinder filled with gently curving layers of glass.

"A lens," Wendy breathed. "Is it for your camera?"

Wordlessly, the boy screwed the device into a hole at the bottom of the accordion-like bellows, then stood back to admire his work.

"That, my dear Wendy Hanson, is the finest photographic enlarger money, or in this case my mom's credit card, can buy."

The girl's mouth dropped open. "It's, it's beautiful," she said. "It looks so . . . elegant." Wendy blinked. She didn't think she'd *ever* hear herself describe something as "elegant."

"Sure is," David agreed, running his hand along the cold, metal contours of the enlarger. "With this baby, I can capture time. I can steal faces right off of people and plaster them up on my walls. I can make a 10-foot daisy or a three-inch skyscraper. Why, I can make you and your sister and everyone on Shadow Creek Ranch smile, or frown, or laugh, or even cry *forever* with this machine and a simple little negative taken from my camera. Whatta ya think of that?"

Wendy, for the first time in her young life, was absolutely speechless. This was better than any ol' alligator. She'd never, ever, ever been introduced to such a marvelous machine—not in New York, not in Montana.

Oh, she'd seen photographs before. Who hadn't? But here, resting on the table right before her eyes, stood the magic behind the images, the power that controlled what everyone remembered of the family vacation or the visit to a faraway land. The girl fairly trembled with the possibilities. Stepping forward she reached out and touched the cylinder, feeling its cold face. "Teach me how to do it," she breathed. "Teach me how to make magic with your machine."

David moved close to his companion, his eyes locked on the enlarger. "Together," he whispered solemnly, "you and I are going to capture moments, snatch events, grab pieces of time like leaves falling from a tree. Then we'll hurry into this very room and print those prisoners trapped by my camera, and we won't stop until the images are perfect, flawless, beautiful."

"Yes, beautiful," the girl repeated, her head nodding slowly. She looked up at her companion. "I'll remember this summer forever."

David lifted his hand and Wendy reached up and smacked her palm against his. "Let's begin with Early," she said.

"Early it is," David nodded, drawing in a deep breath. "He'll be our very first prisoner."

CHAPTER 5

The Power of Another

Over the course of the next few weeks, life at the Station settled into its summer schedule with enthusiasm. The five new members of the working ranch began to realize that this wasn't going to be a simple vacation away from the city, away from the past. Every activity, no matter how spontaneous, seemed to have a purpose built into it.

This was the result of Ms. Cadena's tireless planning sessions with Grandpa Hanson and the other adults during the spring. They had met, sometimes late into the night, to review, discuss, clarify objectives, and encourage each other. They would be dealing with teenagers' futures. Nothing was more important than that.

Joey, Wrangler Barry, and Mr. Hanson kept the secret of the uninvited arrow to themselves, believing that the more people who knew about the incident, the greater chance there'd be to respond in a wrong way. Problem is, they couldn't come up with a right way.

Joey insisted he could handle the situation alone. After hearing of his encounter on the mountain, Mr. Hanson wasn't quite so sure.

"She could've nailed me to a tree," the boy insisted. "But she didn't. I don't think she really wants to hurt nobody. She's just mad and doesn't know what to do about it."

Mr. Hanson finally agreed to give him one more chance. "Then we're calling Crow Agency," he warned.

The summer guests quickly fell into a routine. Lyle and Judy cheerfully went about their household chores, with Samantha as their unofficial helper.

Occasionally, the little girl would stop and stare at the expressionless Judy for a long moment. Then she'd shake her head and busy herself with the task at hand.

Gina's interest in cooking grew, as did her respect for Lizzy Pierce. She'd even presented dishes of her own creation on several occasions. Debbie's description of the girl's first attempt at rice pudding was "unusual, but interesting." Joey smiled gamely at his bean and onion casserole and suggested that it needed a pinch of salt. Wendy said her potato salad tasted like cardboard.

But Gina wasn't deterred. Lizzy assured her that people have different tastes and to not worry about Wendy's reaction one bit. "She's the only person I know who puts catsup on chocolate ice cream," the old woman encouraged.

David's darkroom at the end of the hall was now fully operational. He and his young assistant spent hours stalking the valleys and mountainsides, camera in hand, looking for images to capture and rush to the marvelous machine that waited in the orangish gloom back in the Station.

Together they developed roll after roll of black-and-white film, pouring first one liquid chemical then another into the round, plastic developing tank the boy had brought with him from Seattle. After washing the strips thoroughly in the bathroom sink, David and Wendy examined the negatives over a light table and made contact sheets so they could see their pictures as positive duplicates.

Then with much whispering and earnest discussion, they slipped a selected piece of film into the enlarger and shone the hard-earned likeness onto a large sheet of photographic paper held tightly across the flat base of the device.

Next came the magic, the moment they'd been waiting for. Carefully, oh, so carefully, the paper was submerged in the slightly yellowish liquid in the first of three wide developing trays. Their heads bent low, watching, waiting, searching for a first glimpse of the emerging photograph as the powerful chemicals did their work.

Mysteriously, portions of the picture began to appear. If it was a person or animal that had been photographed, eyes usually materialized before anything else. This might be followed by an ear, or patch of hair.

Then, suddenly, the entire image sprang into view, prompting muffled gasps of joy and shouts of victory to echo down the Station hallway.

"Look at that!" Wendy called. "It's beautiful. It's marvelous. It's—"

"Too dark," David groaned. "We'd better do it again and use eight seconds instead of 10."

But they didn't mind reexposing the image. It gave them a chance to witness the magic all over again.

Alex, on the other hand, wasn't having as much fun.

One bright, warm day frustrated words sounded from the confines of the barn.

"This horse doesn't like me," the teenager announced.

Wrangler Barry looked up from the worktable. "Whadda ya mean, he doesn't like you?"

The boy in the wheelchair reached out and ran a big brush down the side of the chestnut mare. "See? She keeps moving away. I have to unlock my wheels, scoot forward, lock the wheels again, then brush. She moves further. I move further. We end up going around and around like slow-motion ballroom dancers."

Barry chuckled. "Now, what'd I tell you about that?"

"I know, I know. I'm supposed to talk to the dumb animal and brush her with my hand first so she'll get used to me being here."

"So what's the problem?"

Alex shook his head. "I never know what to say to a horse."

"What would you say if she was a beautiful girl?"

The boy paused. "You want me to ask this four-footed hay cruncher for a date?"

Barry rolled his eyes. "Just say nice things like 'Good girl, pretty girl.'"

Alex stared at the horse that stood patiently in front of him. Raising his brush he cooed, "Good girl pretty girl stay put don't move you gorgeous thing you're marvelous you're wonderful I hate your guts."

The animal's tail swung around and knocked the boy's hat off.

"Hey," he cried. "Did you see that? She punched me with her tail. Ain't fair."

Wrangler Barry shook his head. "Alex, what *is* your problem?"

The younger boy's lips tightened. "I'm supposed to be a wrangler and I'm sitting in a wheelchair, *that's* my problem."

Barry shrugged. "Hasn't stopped me."

"Oh, really?" Alex twisted his chair around and moved toward the open door. "I see you looking at us when we go riding in the afternoon. I know what you're feeling. Don't try to play doctor with me."

Barry paused in his work. "You don't hear me complaining, do you?"

"I don't have to hear it, buddy, ol' pal. We're both freaks of nature and always will be."

"THAT'S NOT TRUE!" Wrangler Barry shouted angrily, then regained his composure. "That's not true. We both have to make allowances for our handicaps, but that shouldn't stop us from doing what we want to do."

Alex's eyes narrowed. "It stops us from *being* what we want to *be*. Give it up, cowboy. You can't teach me anything I don't already know. You may be a few years older than I am, but I've had a lot more practice at being a cripple. Just like me, you'll learn what it takes to get by."

"By breaking the law?" the wrangler challenged. "You call that getting by?"

"Hey, I do what I gotta do."

Barry threw down the screwdriver he was holding. It bounced across the top of the workbench, scattering wood shavings and pieces of leather. "You're wrong, Alex! You're wrong to think that way. There are people who want to help you. People who care."

Alex turned sharply. "Maybe for you. Maybe out here on this fancy dude ranch there are people who'll take the time to listen to you rant and rave about how sorry you are for yourself.

"But I ain't got nobody to listen to me. My mom works hard. She's never home. And I ain't exactly mobile sitting in this rotten contraption. So when I feel afraid, when I feel like I'm the only crippled teenager on my block, which I am, I get mad. I do dumb stuff. But it keeps me from losin' it. And I have a little fun in the process.

"So don't think for one minute that showing me how to talk to a horse is going to make my day. Show me how to stop being angry inside every time I see someone run across a baseball field and snag a fly. Show me how to live without being terrified everyday that I'll be left in the middle of nowhere with no one around to push me home.

"You wanna heal me, cowboy? Heal yourself first. Then we'll talk."

Alex angrily maneuvered his chair to the door and slipped outside, his hands and arms straining against the resistance of mud and manure. He floundered 10 feet from the door, unable to move any further.

Wrangler Barry closed his eyes, feeling wet tears creep down his cheeks. The boy's words had cut like a knife, not because they were angry but because they were true.

The horseman lifted his cane from the table and hobbled to the doorway. "Alex," he called, his voice uncertain, "I'm sorry. I really don't know what to do for you . . . or for me. All I know is that I care. The people on this ranch have taught me to care. I can't help myself. They're always talking about God and His love and how we're supposed to share it with others. It makes sense, even though it's not easy sometimes.

"So I guess you're stuck with me. Are you listening? I'm not going to give up on you, Alex. I'm not going to let you go back to San Francisco and continue breaking the law and getting into trouble. The things you do are wrong. I don't want you to do them anymore."

Alex leaned his head against the back of his wheelchair, eyes tightly closed. He felt helpless, a feeling he'd experienced often. Even now, he was stuck, his wheels buried six inches in mud, in front of a horse barn in Montana. There was nothing he could do to help himself.

Angry tears stung his eyes. Why? Why would he have to spend his life depending on other people? Why would he have to be afraid of the simplest trip to town or to school? Why would he always be forced to sit and watch life pass him by, a life filled with people who could laugh, who could hope—who could walk?

The boy felt something hard hit his back and shoulder. Looking down he saw one end of a thick rope resting in his lap. "Tie it low on your chair," a determined voice called.

Glancing back he noticed Wrangler Barry slowly swinging the chestnut mare around inside the barn workshop.

Alex bent and fastened the stout cord to the seat frame of his wheelchair. Barry painfully wrapped his end of the rope around the horse's neck. Then with a soft command, the wrangler, leaning heavily on his cane, guided the large animal back toward the stalls.

Alex felt the rope tighten, then he found himself moving slowly across the damp, muddy ground. In moments he was slipping along the solid boards that formed the horse barn's floor.

Unfastening the rope, he saw Wrangler Barry hobbling in his direction. The two paused and looked at each other for a long moment, understanding that they'd just accomplished something quite unusual. A person who couldn't strain on a rope had just pulled another person who couldn't walk, out of the mud. All they had done was borrow the power of another.

Barry smiled shyly. "Not bad for a couple freaks of nature, huh?"

"What did you say to the horse to make her do that?" Alex questioned.

The older boy shrugged. "Just two words. 'Help us.'"

Alex grinned a tired grin. "You sure know how to talk to horses." Then he looked down at the floor. "Would you teach me?"

Barry studied his companion as the soft sound of shuffling hooves on fresh straw drifted from the far end of the stalls. He lifted his hands and spoke quietly. "I may not know how to do it right."

The boy in the wheelchair nodded. "I need your help, Barry. Where else can I go to find someone who speaks horse?"

* * *

Lizzy looked up from her bread dough in surprise when she saw who'd just walked into her kitchen. "Hey, Gina, aren't you going with the group to visit Red Stone? They're about to leave."

The girl ambled to the sink window and glanced out toward the pasture where Joey and Wrangler Barry were making sure the ranch's young riders were properly mounted on their eager steeds. Alex could be heard calling out instructions from atop Lightning.

"Nah. I'm not in the mood to ride today," Gina sighed.

"Well, that's OK," Lizzy smiled. "You can keep me

company. Grandma Hanson went to Bozeman with Tyler, and Grandpa Hanson's up in the mountains, visiting our neighbors, John and Merrilee Dawson. I'm stuck here at home, baking some bread for tomorrow. Wanna help?"

Gina grinned and twisted one of the knobs on the faucet. "I was hoping you'd say that," she replied, lathering her hands with soap. "It's not that I don't like horses. I just didn't feel like bouncing around all day."

"I understand," Lizzy nodded. "I'm not much of a cowgirl myself. Guess I'm gettin' too old for such goin's on."

Gina powdered her fingers with flour and thrust them into a large lump of wheat dough. "You're not old. You're . . . you're experienced in years."

Lizzy paused. "What a lovely way of putting it. Thanks."

The teenager bent to her work. "Do you have any children, Lizzy?"

"Nope. Never did. My young, dashing husband was killed in the Second World War. Airplane pilot. Shot down over France."

Gina shook her head. "That's sad. I'm sorry."

"So was I. So sorry, I guess, that I never married again. Kinda foolish of me—trying to stay faithful to a dead man."

The teenager squeezed another lump of dough and slapped it on the table. "You would've been a great mother," she said. "You make kids laugh. And you're patient."

"Had to get that way pretty fast when I began

teaching school in New York City. Without a sense of humor and the patience of Job, you'd be climbing the walls before the second bell.

"Then I met Joey when his parents moved into the same apartment as mine." The speaker paused. "Joey. Now there's a good kid. Heart as big as all of Montana and Wyoming combined. 'Cept he didn't know it at the time. He figured he had to be a tough guy, so he was. After little Samantha showed up in his life, he had a real problem. How do you play the tough street hood and take care of a tiny child at the same time? It was a battle for him."

Gina smiled. "My mother is like you."

The old woman lifted her lump of dough and dropped it into a deep baking pan. "Which one?" she asked, not looking up.

"My *real* one, of course. She's rich. And very smart."

"Really? Have you talked to her?"

Gina shook her head. "Nah. A couple years ago I convinced my adopted parents to help me locate her. I wrote her a letter, but she didn't reply. Too busy making money for us."

"Us?"

"Yeah. The way I see it, she's going to save up until she has enough in the bank for us to travel around the world together. Egypt, India, Africa. We'll have a great time. She's not far—" Gina hesitated. "I mean, she's president of a big corporation. Tells everyone what to do. But she loves me. I just know it. And she's got plans for us." The girl chuckled playfully. "After all, I *am* her daughter."

Lizzy slipped several bread pans into the oven and adjusted the temperature control. "I'm sure she thinks of you often."

The two were silent for a moment. Outside the window, the last of the riders disappeared from view as the happy group headed for Freedom Mountain. Samantha could be heard playing with Pueblo by the footbridge, encouraging the dog to climb a tree to see if there were any eggs in the nest clinging to "the third limb from the right, the one with the bump on it."

"We're going to be very happy together," Gina added softly. "She'll understand me. She'll treat me like an adult, not a child."

Lizzy sprayed a thin layer of cooking oil on a pan and set it down gently. "Have you told the McClintocks about your dream?"

"It's not a dream," the girl tensed. "It's real."

"Don't you think they should know what you're planning? I mean, they've invested a lot in you—not only time, but money, too. They have the right to know when you'll be leaving."

Gina nodded slowly. "They know I'm not happy living with them anymore."

"But why, Gina?" Lizzy pressed. "Please explain to me what it is you don't like about the McClintocks." Seeing her companion's face begin to cloud, she added quickly, "Because, they might want to know so they won't make the same mistakes with their next daughter."

106

The teenager's expression softened. "Perhaps you're right. I guess they deserve at least that much."

Lizzy closed her eyes momentarily, knowing how close she'd come to making her young friend angry again.

"OK. I'll tell you." The girl sighed as she walked to the window and gazed out into the late-morning sunshine. "When I was little, everything was fine. They treated me great. We'd go on camping trips to the Adirondacks, drive through New England in the fall to see the colorful leaves, spend a week at the beach every summer."

"And they stopped doing that?"

"No. But for the last couple years they've gotten bossy, you know, telling me everything I'm supposed to do. 'Clean up your room . . . lengthen your skirt . . . don't hang around with so-and-so . . . be home by 9:00 . . . don't watch that video.'" The girl straightened. "That's not love. That's dictatorship. I'm not free to do what I want anymore."

Lizzy nodded. "So you do things like shoplifting and getting in trouble with the law to show them who's boss, right?"

"You bet. No one's going to rule my life."

The old woman dropped another lump of dough into a pan and carried it to the oven. "We had a girl here last summer whose father abused her, physically and otherwise. Project Youth Revival arranged for her and her sister to have a new home with a caring couple. She writes to Debbie, boasting about how her new parents do the very same things you're talking about, except this girl is amazed that two people could love her so much they'd bother noticing the length of her skirts and who her friends were. Why do you think you and she see things so differently?"

Gina was silent for a long moment. When she spoke, her words were cold. "I'm not concerned about what other girls may or may not think. I just know there are going to be some changes in my life. Very soon, too."

With that she turned and walked quickly from the room, leaving Lizzy standing, her hands covered with flour, by the open oven.

* * *

Red Stone's smile broadened when he saw Joey and the others emerge from the forest and ride to the entrance of the cave.

"Welcome," the old Indian called as Debbie waved. "Welcome to my mountain."

Joey dismounted and hurried over to his friend. "I've brought you some more listeners for your stories," he grinned. "Think you might have some ready for us?"

Red Stone nodded. "Always have story for boy and girl."

Judy and Lyle slipped from their saddles and tied their horses to a tree limb as they'd been taught. "Nice to meet you," Lyle said, extending his hand. "I ain't never met a real-live Indian before."

Red Stone looked over at Joey. "This boy talk funny. Like you, only different."

The young wrangler laughed. "He's from Texas and I'm from New York. I guess we both have pretty weird accents—at least that's what Montana people say."

Judy stood and looked at the Indian thoughtfully as Lyle grinned. "My cousin here ain't never seen an Indian before, either," Lyle offered. "We've met lots of Mexicans, being from Texas and all, but no Indians."

Judy blinked and continued staring. Red Stone returned her gaze. "Does girl know how to talk?" he asked.

"Sure she does," Lyle laughed. "But she likes to save up her words for special occasions. Then she rattles off like a train at a crossing. Yak, yak, yak. Can't shut her up for love nor money."

Click. The old Indian turned to see Wendy and a boy peering from behind a camera. "Did you get 'em?" Wendy asked.

"Yup," David nodded. "The sun's just in the right place too, sorta back-lighting him and Joey."

"You opened up enough for the shadowed areas, didn't you?"

"Yeah. Gave it a full stop. Should be a keeper."

Red Stone nudged Joey. "What Wendy and boy talk about?"

The teenager grinned. "That's David, one of our guests. He's teaching Wendy how to take pictures, and they're making a photo album, all about Shadow Creek Ranch. I'll bring you a copy when it's done."

Wendy waved. "Hi, Red Stone. Where's the best place to get a good view of Mount Blackmore?"

The old Indian pointed to his left. "Up there," he said. Wendy and David hurried away, camera and exposure meter in hand.

"What am I, a permanent fixture up here?" Alex lifted his arms and dropped them with a sigh.

Joey and Lyle hurried to Lightning's side. "Sorry 'bout that, Alex," Joey chuckled. "We forgot all about you."

"Well, I guess so," Alex teased. "But Wrangler Barry's teachin' me how to put up with just such incompetence. He says I should politely express my needs. I'm pretty good at expressin', but the polite part still could use some work."

The two boys gently carried their friend into the cave and deposited him on a pile of blankets. "You're doin' just fine," Lyle encouraged. "You haven't even hit on ol' Debbie for goin' on 20 minutes now."

"And I appreciate that," another voice called from the group of horses. The girl in question walked up and gave Red Stone a friendly hug. She paused, a shadow crossing her face. "You losin' some weight, Red Stone? And you look just a little pale."

The old man grinned. "No, no! Don't you know that *White* man is paleface? Not Indian. We're redskin."

Debbie giggled. "So what color do you get when you're not feeling good?"

Red Stone thought for a moment. "Pink," he said. "Yes. That's right. Pink."

"Well, then," Debbie pressed, looking into the kind eyes of the old Indian. "You're looking a little pink. Maybe these cold nights up here are gettin' to ya. Why don't you let my grandpa take you to see the doctor? Perhaps he can make you . . . red again."

Red Stone laughed. "I'm strong as grizzly. Don't worry. Plenty look after me."

Just then Wendy and David returned from their short journey to the overlook. "Sun's not right," the boy sighed. "We'll try again later."

Everyone settled themselves at the mouth of the cave as Red Stone poked a stick into a small fire. Although it had been warm in the valley, Freedom Mountain rose to where the air was always cooler, especially to the old Indian whose body was worn by years.

"Tell us about Shadow Creek when it wasn't Shadow Creek," Wendy encouraged.

Red Stone nodded. "You mean Valley of Laughing Waters?" He opened his mouth to continue but paused as another person entered the cave. Joey looked up to see Plenty standing silhouetted against the bright forest sky.

"Come, Great-granddaughter!" the old Indian called happily. He wanted all to understand his invitation. "Sit by me and listen. I tell about my father's valley to my new friends." His hand swept the air. "They have journeyed up Freedom Mountain to listen."

Joey watched the girl slip her quiver from her shoulder and lean her bow against the cave wall. "Whatever you say, Great-grandfather." She moved among the gathering and knelt beside him. Never once did her eyes glance in Joey's direction.

The young horseman studied the girl thought-fully. What would she do next? What plan was cir-culating in her mind even as she sat beside the old storyteller there in the cave, listening to adven-tures from long ago?

The afternoon passed quickly, too quickly for the visitors on Red Stone's mountain. They were carried, again and again, to another time, when this part of the Gallatins rang with the joyous voices of children. These children were members of the Mountain Crow tribe, a people honored to be overseers of this corner of nature's pure and unspoiled wilderness.

The old Indian drew his listeners from the pres-ent and gave them front-row seats to a way of life that had vanished forever under the uncaring tread of modern civilization. Lyle, Judy, Alex, David, and the others sat spellbound as the age-worn voice of their guide painted graphic work-pictures of the way life used to be. In beautiful detail, he told how his own laughter used to mingle with that of other tribal children as they splashed through mountain streams and lay dreaming under summer stars.

Evening shadows were beginning to creep across the land as Joey and the others bade farewell to their old friend and turned their horses homeward. Plenty stood with her great-grandfather at the entrance to the cave, silent, her expression emotion-less. Joey could feel her hatred, even though she had tried to act civil for her great-grandfather's sake.

As they rode away, the young wrangler glanced one last time over his shoulder. Plenty was looking directly at him. He waved. She did not respond.

* * *

A few days later, the phone rang in Mr. Hanson's office, as it often did during the day. He picked up the receiver and pressed it to his ear, his other hand still tapping on his computer keys.

"Hanson here," he said.

The voice on the other end of the line sounded friendly. "Mr. Hanson of Shadow Creek Ranch?" it questioned.

"One and the same," the lawyer sang out.

"I just wanted you to know that your girl got off safe and sound."

"I beg your pardon?"

"Your girl. She left right on time. Put her on board myself."

The lawyer's hand froze above the keyboard. "What are you talking about?"

The voice paused. "You are Tyler Hanson of Shadow Cr—"

"Yes, yes. That's me. What girl?"

"She said you'd made the arrangements, Mr. Hanson. Even brought a letter signed by you. Has your business address and phone number on it."

"Wait a minute, friend," Mr. Hanson chuckled, running his fingers through his hair. "You've lost me. Where are you calling from?"

"Bozeman. The train station. I put your girl on the 4:00 limited to Denver, just as you requested. My company has a policy of calling to confirm when

113

a minor is placed on board."

The lawyer's mouth dropped open. "What was her name?" he gasped.

The voice on the line hesitated.

"HER NAME!" Mr. Hanson commanded.

"Gina. Gina Hanson, your daughter."

The man slammed the phone down on its cradle and bolted for the door. Reaching the top of the stairs, he shouted, "Mrs. Pierce! MRS. PIERCE! Is Gina with you?"

"No, Tyler," came the reply from downstairs. "I think she went to town with Debbie earlier this afternoon." Lizzy appeared at the bottom step. "Whatever is the matter?"

"I just got a call from the train station telling me that my daughter, Gina Hanson, was put aboard the 4:00 limited to Denver."

"Oh, my; oh, my!" the woman gasped. "What are we going to do?"

Mr. Hanson lifted his hands. "First Joey disappeared last fall, now Gina. Doesn't anyone want to *stay* on this ranch?!" Racing back into his office he shouted over his shoulder, "I'm calling Ruth Cadena. Find my dad. Looks like we've got another teenager to track down."

CHAPTER 6

The Mistake

♦ ♦ ♦

Traffic jammed the streets, and harried pedestrians jostled for position along downtown sidewalks and crossing zones. Car horns blared their drivers' impatience at busy intersections and parking lots.

Motors raced, trucks and taxis inched forward, and the smell of burnt diesel fuel mixed with the odor of strong coffee. Gina moved with the flow of people, past small restaurants that cowered at the bases of towering glass-and-steel structures.

It was morning. Her long rail journey had come to an end. The girl had watched the sunrise through a dusty window at Union Station and was now making her way along 8th Avenue toward an address she'd memorized months before.

Gina hadn't bothered to eat breakfast. She was far too excited. Today was going to be the beginning of a whole new life for her, a life of freedom with the woman who had brought her into this world, a woman whose face she'd imagined a million times.

A street number glowed in golden letters across

the glass entrance to a tall office building on the corner of 8th and Broadway. This was it! This was the correct address. To make sure her excitement wasn't clouding her mind, she dug into her change purse and found the paper with those magic words scrawled across them. L & R Media Productions, 49789 8th Avenue, Denver, Colorado. Gina smiled. She knew the "L" stood for Lynda, her birth mother's first name.

The young girl exited the elevator at the eighteenth floor and stood looking around the tastefully decorated lobby. "May I help you?" The receptionist smiled up at her.

"Yes," Gina said, returning the smile. "I'm looking for Lynda Ellis. She's the president of L & R Media Productions."

The receptionist nodded. "Does she know you're coming? I mean, do you have an appointment?"

"No. It's a . . . surprise visit."

"Ms. Ellis doesn't get too many young visitors," the woman reported. Leaning forward she pointed as she spoke. "Head down that hallway to the end, turn right, and Ms. Ellis's secretary will be sitting behind the desk by the window. She'll find out if she can see you."

"Oh, she'll see me," Gina grinned confidently. Turning to leave, she paused. "Do you work for her?"

The receptionist laughed. "Young lady, everyone on this floor works for Lynda Ellis."

Gina smiled. "She must be a wonderful boss."

There was a short pause. "She gets the job done,"

the receptionist said flatly.

The hallway was lined with office doors, each with a different name and title printed neatly on the frosted glass—Adam Tarrance: West Coast Sales; Elaine LeClair: Accounting; George Digman: Photography; Samuel Aikens: Copy Editing; Sharon Daily: Desktop Publishing. On and on they went; musicians, sound recordists, videographers, editors, writers. Every few seconds a door would burst open and someone would rush by as if on an urgent mission.

The secretary's desk waited right where the receptionist said it would be. A woman was furiously typing at a computer as Gina approached.

"Yes?" she asked, not looking up.

"I'd like to see Ms. Ellis, please."

The secretary chuckled. "Take a number."

"What?"

"Everyone wants to see Ms. Ellis."

Gina frowned. "No. I'm not here on business."

The secretary pressed some keys on her computer keyboard and a laser printer whirred to life by her elbow. "Today's not a good day. Try next Wednesday."

Gina stepped forward. "You don't understand. I've got to see her right away."

The secretary stopped working and studied the young visitor who stood before her desk. "Look, she's busy. She's always busy. Leave your number and I'll have her call you later. Besides, auditions have closed."

"But I'm not auditioning for anything. I just want to see her. I've come a long—"

"Listen, I don't mean to be rude, but Ms. Ellis is an extremely busy woman." The secretary pointed in the direction of a thick, wooden door across the small lobby. "She's in a committee right now, trying to figure out how one of her pet projects went 'way over budget.' She doesn't have time for social calls from nice young women. So if you'll just come back in a few days, she might be able to see you. OK?"

Gina fought back a strong urge to scream out her demands. "But I have to—"

"Thanks for stopping by. Now, you must leave."

The girl nodded slowly and turned. After walking a few paces she glanced back just as the phone rang. The secretary picked up the receiver and began a heated conversation with someone on the other end of the line. So engrossed was she in her call that she didn't see the young visitor crack open the big, wooden door and slip inside.

Gina found herself in a small hallway lined with award plaques and autographed photos of celebrities. The girl recognized the pictures of many Hollywood and television actors along the brightly-lit gallery.

"What do you mean, you had to shoot another day?" A woman's voice drifted from the archway at the end of the hall. "Cost us $15,000 and we were already over budget."

"We had no choice," a man's voice pleaded. "It rained."

"It's not supposed to rain in Los Angeles in June. I think it's the law." Gina heard people laugh.

"The studios were booked solid," the unseen man

continued. "We had to stay on location for an additional day and that's that. Period. What's done is done. It was either shoot or postpone the product launch date two weeks. Marketing would've had my liver for lunch."

Gina heard the woman sigh. "Just plan a little better from now on, OK? We're in this business to *make* money, not spend it. Now, everyone get outta here and do some magic with the WebCore account. We'll try to recover our losses by milking them for another $50,000, but don't put me in this position again or *I'll* take a few bites of your liver."

The girl heard chairs bump and the muffled voices of people approaching. She ducked behind a large plastic plant beside a statue of a lion; she waited as eight or nine sets of highly polished shoes shuffled by. Then all was quiet.

Peeking around the plant, Gina could just make out the slender form of the woman seated at a wide, expensive-looking desk. She had tied her dark brown hair up behind her head, leaving long, curving strands that cascaded over her ears and forehead. She wore a red dress, tightly fitted. The sun's rays, piercing the long, lacy curtains with warm, morning light struck the side of her face, illuminating it with a soft glow.

She was beautiful, with smooth skin and practiced grace, just like Gina had imagined.

A couch stood nearby, and an overstuffed chair. A rolled-up newspaper balanced on the broad back of the chair, probably left by one of the employees who'd just departed.

Gina stepped from behind the plant and stood in full view, staring in wonder at the president of L & R Media Productions.

"Who are you?" the woman asked when she saw the teenager in the archway.

"I'm Gina."

"Auditions were yesterday. We'll let you know when—"

"I'm Gina," the girl repeated. "Your daughter."

The woman paused, then smiled. "I don't have a daughter."

"Yes, you do. Me."

The woman reached for the phone, then hesitated. "What makes you think that?"

Gina stepped forward. "I checked. This is the address, and you're Lynda Ellis. That means you're my mother."

The woman rose slowly and walked around her desk until she stood before it. "How old are you?"

"Fourteen. Almost 15. I'll be 15 in September."

Gina could see her companion make some quick, mental calculations. Suddenly, she saw her expression harden. "Why have you come here?"

"Because," Gina replied, smiling, "I want to live with you."

The woman laughed out loud. "You want to live with me? Listen, . . . whoever you are. I want you to understand something. You're not a part of my life. You never were."

"You carried me inside you."

THE MISTAKE

The woman glanced out the window. "Fourteen years ago I made a mistake. Then I fixed that mistake by turning it over to the proper authorities. What's done is done. Now, go back to wherever you came from and leave me alone."

The words hit Gina like flying pieces of glass. She almost staggered under their impact.

"You're my mother! You carried me for nine months and then gave birth to me. I'm not a mistake. I'm a person, a person who loves you and wants to—"

"I don't have time for this," the woman interrupted, glancing at her watch and turning back to her desk. "You mustn't come here anymore. Please leave."

"But Mother—"

"DON'T CALL ME THAT! Never . . . call me that." The woman turned around, her eyes narrow, cold. "You have no right to barge into my office and demand anything of me. I did what's best for you 14 years ago. It's still best. Nothing has changed."

Gina braced herself under the full weight of the woman's words. "But you love me," she encouraged. "I know you do. We can be happy together. We can travel, see things. I can tell you what's in my heart. You can listen and hold me when—"

Gina stopped talking as she realized her words were not being accepted by the lovely lady standing behind the desk.

"I'm not your mother," the woman said firmly. "I may have given birth to you, but I'm not your mother. I never will be. Do you understand?"

Tears moistened the corners of Gina's eyes. There was nothing between them. No warmth. No understanding. It was as if they were separated by a bottomless canyon, uncrossable, unchangeable, unseen.

"Don't you care for me just a little?" she whispered. "Don't you ever think about me, how I'm doin', what I look like?"

"That's not my responsibility," the woman replied. "I gave up that privilege when I let you go. I refused to hold you in my arms then. And I refuse to hold you in my thoughts now. So, you see, as far as I'm concerned, you don't exist. Believe me, it's best for both of us."

The woman moved across the room and brushed by the teenager without looking at her. She continued out into the hallway and paused at the big, wooden door. "You must go now," Gina heard her say. "Don't be here when I return."

The room fell silent except for the soft whistle of air passing through the air-conditioner ducts somewhere overhead. Gina walked to the window and stared out across the city to the Rocky Mountains beyond. Some summits still carried their winter coats, the snow looking as cold and distant as the woman had been.

The girl trembled slightly, too sad to cry. Her dreams had been crushed, her carefully planned future destroyed. She'd lived each day in preparation for a new life with the woman who worked at the corner of 8th Avenue and Broadway. Now she felt terribly alone, cast aside like so much rubbish—unwanted by the very woman who had given her life.

"Gina?" A soft voice called from the doorway. The girl didn't turn.

"We're here, Gina. Both of us. We came as soon as we heard."

Mr. and Mrs. McClintock stood together at the far end of the office, their expressions shaped by the deep concern that filled their hearts. "Are you all right?"

Gina closed her eyes as a sob rocked her body. "Do you hate me now?" she asked, her words barely audible.

"No!" came the quick reply. "No. We could never hate you. We love you, more than you'll ever understand."

Gina turned slowly, looking down at the thick carpet at her feet. "She said I was a mistake. She said she didn't ever think about me."

Mrs. McClintock began to cry. "You're not a mistake, Gina. You're a treasure, to us, to our home."

The man stepped forward. "We're not perfect parents," he said, fighting back his own tears. "But we're there when you need us. We never had such a wonderful little girl before. We just don't want anything bad to happen to you. That's why we try so hard to keep you safe from the pain we know waits all around."

The girl allowed her gaze to rise until she was looking into the kind, loving eyes of the couple by the door. "Will you forgive me?" she whispered. "Will you forgive me for causing so much trouble?"

Gina rushed forward and fell into waiting arms. They cried together for a long time, lost in the unspeakable joy that a parent feels when a child accepts the love they offer, and when a child learns just how far a parent's heart will reach to forgive.

* * *

The cozy den was silent as Mr. Hanson finished his report. It was evening. Crickets sang and buzzed outside in the darkness. The quarter moon hung just above the trees, its silver light touching the ripples playing along the banks of Shadow Creek.

He'd just gotten off the phone with the McClintocks, who were back in Rochester with their daughter. Lizzy reached up and wiped her eyes with a handkerchief. "This whole episode reminds me of something Grandpa Hanson said earlier this year during one of our planning sessions with Ms. Cadena."

"I remember," Debbie nodded, smiling over at the old man sitting by the hearth. "You said we were all like children lost in a world of sin with no one to love us. Then God offers to adopt us, so we can be part of a loving family again."

Joey sighed. "I know what it's like to feel alone and rejected, like Gina. But I also remember how great it felt when Dizzy offered to be my friend and when Mr. H chased me down in that old warehouse and said he'd never leave me again. Believe you me, there's nothin' like it in the whole world."

Grandpa Hanson glanced about the room, letting his gaze pause at each of the ranch's remaining summer guests. "Listen, guys. I don't care what kind of mess you're in. Doesn't matter what you've done, or where you've gone, or who you've hurt. God says, 'Come back home to Me. You're always welcome at My supper table. And if you'll listen, I'll teach you how to avoid trouble, how to right the wrongs you've done, how to bring peace back into your heart.'" The old man sighed. "So few people take Him up on His offer. They just keep on hurting themselves, and others, until the law, or their own guilt, sentences them to a lifetime of sorrow."

David fingered the controls of his ever-present camera. "The other day Wendy and I were up in the mountains, past Merrilee. We were looking for a small patch of nodding onions—you know, the little pink jobs? Debbie had said wildlife really likes 'em and we were hoping to see a bear or elk or something.

"Anyway, while we were huntin' around, we heard this chirp . . . chirp . . . chirping coming from a bush. We figured we might get a shot of some baby birds for our book, so we headed in that direction. On the way we saw this pile of feathers on the ground, like there'd been a fight—and the bird lost. We looked up the feather patterns in our bird field guide and decided it was a horned lark, or at least it used to be.

"When we got to the nest, guess what? Baby horned larks. It made us sad to think that the mother bird wouldn't be bringing breakfast to the nest anymore. The babies were way too small to save, so we had to leave 'em. I can still hear them chirping and chirping, calling for their mom as we left the area. Gina's story sorta reminds me of that."

"At least Gina has a new mother and father who love her," Lyle added. "Some kids don't."

Alex nodded. "Seems to me that bein' a mother is more than giving birth to a baby. It means stickin' by that kid, day in and day out. It's lovin' him even when he does something stupid like go off on his own like Gina did. Guess she didn't know just how good things were for her back in Rochester. Somethin' tells me she's kinda figuring that out now.

"You know, I learned something awhile back." He glanced at Wrangler Barry. "I learned that you shouldn't try to do everything alone. You need parents, or at least someone to help you with your problems. Know what I mean? Some people are smarter than you are, although in my case, that may be hard to believe." Barry grinned as the boy continued. "And the smartest thing that you can do, is shut your mouth and listen. It's amazing what can happen."

Lyle lifted his hand. "You know what I'm going to do when I get back to Texas? I'm going to give my mom and dad a great big kiss right on their noses." Everyone giggled. "No, really. I am. This whole thing with Gina made me appreciate what they do for me. It's true they get on my nerves from time to time, probably always will. But instead of going off and doing something dumb, I'm going to stop and think. At least they're there. They may not be perfect, but neither am I. Why should I get all bent out of shape when they screw up and then expect them to be loving and forgiving when I do something really dumb? I gotta be fair. Yeah, that's it. I gotta be fair with my parents. That means letting the other guy make mistakes without calling in the National Guard. Know what I mean?"

"Yes," Judy said firmly. Everyone gasped as the girl who'd not said one audible word since arriving on the ranch smiled over at her cousin. She nodded and looked around the room. "Must be fair."

Lyle threw up his hands. "See what I mean? Once she gets started, you can't get a word in edgewise."

The den exploded with laughter as Grandpa Hanson shook his head and smiled broadly. He knew something was stirring in the hearts of the teenagers who had, as expected, become part of the Shadow Creek Ranch family. The seeds had been planted. Now it was up to the Holy Spirit to help them grow.

CHAPTER 7

Light of the New Day

🦅 🦅 🦅

Dawn was just beginning to tinge the eastern sky when Plenty stirred. She'd been dreaming. At least, she thought she had. There was such a feeling of joy filling her body that she closed her eyes again, trying to recapture the fading images, but it was too late. Sleep had slipped away, like the night beyond the entrance to her great-grandfather's cave.

Her companion coughed a quiet cough, the sound rattling in his throat like pebbles in a jar. It was a comforting sound, like the creak of an old floor or squeak of a back door in a home lived in for many years.

The weeks had flown by, days tumbling over each other in rapid succession. She'd found her frequent walks with Red Stone had become more relaxed, more enjoyable. His gentle words, patient training, and constant encouragement were beginning to chip away at her stony heart.

His often repeated stories began to take on fresh meaning as she experienced the mountains firsthand.

When he spoke of the things of nature, she didn't have to imagine them anymore. She'd seen the graceful gait of a white-tailed deer. She'd heard the throaty trumpet of the bull elk, listened to the clatter of pronghorn sheep's hooves on slabs of granite, watched red squirrels playing tag high in the forest canopy, and witnessed the silent flight of the great horned owl.

From her perch above Shadow Creek Ranch, she'd seen the summer guests take their leave amid happy calls and tearful waves. They'd driven away in a little red minivan, trailing a cloud of dust in their wake.

The valley seemed empty to her now. She went less often to sit and gaze down at the Station.

Red Stone rose on one elbow as he did each morning, then stumbled to his feet, taking a little longer than usual.

"Are you OK, Great-grandfather?" Plenty asked, yawning.

"Oh, yes. I'm fine. Just a little stiff, that's all." The girl reluctantly slipped from beneath her warm blanket and helped her great-grandfather to the mouth of the cave. Then she took her usual place at his feet. The morning ritual, something she was now very familiar with, was about to begin. She understood it was part of Red Stone's life, and although she didn't exactly feel the need to greet the morning sun when it decided to rise, she'd play along if only to keep him happy.

As the first rays of the sun pierced the dark sky, setting the horizon on fire, Red Stone lifted his arms. "Master of the Morning," he sang out, his voice a little more labored than usual. "I greet you. I welcome you." The man swayed and caught himself. Plenty tensed as he continued. "Guide my steps during your . . . during your journey across . . . the sky."

"Great-grandfather. What's wrong?"

"Bless my day . . . my day . . ."

The old man's right arm slammed into his chest as his knees buckled, almost toppling him.

"GREAT-GRANDFATHER! WHAT'S WRONG?"

"And my. . . my heart . . . be filled . . . be filled—"

The words choked in Red Stone's throat as he stumbled backward into the cave, weaving drunkenly, bumping against stone walls. Plenty screamed as the frail, aged body tumbled into a twisted heap by the fire. The man's face was ash-white, his eyes wide with terror.

"WHAT IS IT?" Plenty shrieked, rushing to Red Stone's side. "WHAT IS IT, GREAT-GRANDFATHER?"

The old man jerked in agony, his hand gripping the young girl's arm. "Plenty! PLENTY!"

"I'm here. I'M HERE! What's the matter? What's happening?"

Red Stone closed his eyes tightly as stabbing pains racked his chest and limbs. His face trembled, teeth grinding together, sounding like sandpaper digging into wood. The torturing agony eased just long enough for him to whisper, "Get help."

In one quick movement, Plenty gathered her bow and arrows and was out of the cave, her feet a blur over the frosty ground. She ran faster than she'd ever run before, arms pumping, legs pounding the earth. The path turned into a flowing river of movement, colors blending together, details lost in the rush.

The girl's heart hammered against her ribs, not only from the extreme exertion but also from the fear of what was happening back at the cave. Red Stone had been growing weaker during the last couple days. Plenty had thought it was just a touch of the flu. Now she knew it was something much more serious, much more deadly.

Her breath was coming in great heaves when she arrived at the overlook. All was quiet in the valley. Nothing moved, except the gentle sparkle of the creek as it threaded its way beside the pasture and past the large, white way station resting far beyond the cottonwoods.

With trembling hands, Plenty slipped an arrow from her quiver and placed it between her teeth. Reaching up she gathered several strands of hair and yanked hard, closing her eyes at the sharp pain.

Twisting the long fibers around the middle of the shaft, she tied a quick knot. Then she slipped the arrow into the bow.

Back, back, back she pulled, the wooden weapon straining under the powerful tension the girl placed on it. Her mind calculated the distances, the winds, the drift, the vast sea of space that separated her from the ranch in the valley. Then, with one last tug on the string, she let the arrow fly.

Up, up, up it sailed, silent, free, piercing the cool mountain air like a rocket fired into space. But the girl didn't watch it for long. Another arrow was quickly jammed between her teeth, another length of hair was yanked from her head. Even before the first missile slammed into the thick, wooden door of the barn a second was already arching through the sky, its smooth, polished skin glistening in the early morning light.

THUMP!

Joey jumped as the sound rattled the horse barn, causing him to drop the bucket of oats he was carrying.

"Not again," he moaned, glancing in Wrangler Barry's direction. "That Plenty just doesn't give up. She's beginning to get on my nerves. She won't talk to me, won't—"

THUMP!

"Give me a break!" the boy called angrily as he rushed to the door and flung it open. "So you can shoot a barn," he shouted out across the pasture. "Big deal."

"Wait a minute." Barry hurried over to his companion's side, eying the two arrows jutting from the wooden planks. "Look at them. They're at an incredible angle, like they dropped out of the sky."

Joey reached up and retrieved one of the shafts and held it out in front of him. "And what's this? Looks like hair or something tied to the middle."

Barry gasped. "Get your grandfather. Quickly!"

"Why?" Joey questioned, moving obediently in the direction of the pasture gate.

"The hair tied around the arrow. I read about that in a book on Indian lore. It means something . . . something bad has happened."

Joey broke into a run. Strange, he thought. The arrow had arrived at such an extreme angle. It must have been shot from somewhere far away, somewhere high— He skidded to a stop and spun around. Somewhere like the overlook!

The morning sun glared down with brilliant rays. Squinting, he searched the ring of mountains to the east, looking for the pattern of rocks and trees that marked the spot where he knew Red Stone's path ended at the lip of a towering granite formation.

Then he saw her. A lone figure standing against the distant sky, arms waving frantically, desperately, back and forth. He couldn't see Plenty's expression. He didn't have to. Her movements said it all. Something was terribly wrong on Freedom Mountain.

"GRANDPA HANSON!" Joey screamed, racing up the steps. "Come quickly. Plenty needs help!"

The old man stumbled from the kitchen where he'd been helping his wife prepare breakfast.

"What's the matter, Joey?" he shouted.

"Red Stone! Maybe something's happened to Red Stone! He must be hurt or sick."

Grandpa Hanson turned. "I'll call the doctor in Gallatin Gateway. If he takes the logging road behind Blackmore, he can be at the cave in 45 minutes."

"Right!" Joey called, heading back toward the front door. "I'm taking Tar Boy. You come in the truck."

The boy exploded from the Station and flew down the steps. He pressed his fingers between his lips and created a piercing whistle. Tar Boy's head jerked up and the stallion immediately galloped away from the ranch herd at the far end of the pasture. In seconds, the powerful horse and his rider were thundering up the long driveway, filling the quiet valley with the pounding of hooves.

Wrangler Barry waved his good arm in the air and shouted, "Hurry, Joey! HURRY!"

Plenty was waiting at the cave when the black horse finally burst from the woods and slid to a stop. Joey was off his mount and running even before the animal had come to a complete halt.

"What is it?" he shouted. "What's the matter?"

"My great-grandfather. Something's wrong. He stopped breathing right before you got here."

Joey hurried into the cave. One look told the story. Wordlessly he dropped to the ground beside the man.

"Red Stone!" he shouted, shaking the old Indian's shoulders. "Red Stone! Can you hear me?" There was no response. Joey repeated the question. Nothing.

Joey tilted Red Stone's head back slightly and pressed his mouth against his friend's lips. He blew firmly, filling the prone victim's lungs with air. Red Stone's chest rose and fell with each breath.

Then the boy carefully measured a short space from the man's top chest bone to a spot over his left breast. Placing one hand over the other, Joey pushed down—once, twice, three times, four times, five times. Then he bent and breathed into Red Stone's mouth once again.

This he did several times before shouting, "Breathe or pump?"

"What?" Plenty questioned, her hands trembling.

"Breathe or pump?" Joey shouted again, his voice raspy from the exertion. "Which one do you want to do? Come on, Plenty. I need your help."

"Breathe. I'll breathe."

Joey positioned himself where he could get the best leverage and continued pressing down onto the prone man's chest. Plenty sealed Red Stone's nostrils with her fingers as she'd seen Joey do and began forcing breaths of air into her great-grandfather's lungs.

"They taught us how to do this back in East Village, at my high school," the boy gasped, his arms pumping rhythmically. "Glad I showed up that week."

Plenty fought back tears as she worked to keep oxygen flowing into the old man's lungs. "Is he going to die?"

"I don't know," Joey answered, his voice uneven as he continued pressing down on Red Stone's chest. "He was always telling us that the heart of the warrior is strong. I sure hope he's right. Grandpa Hanson and the others should be here soon. Doctor's on his way, too. We just gotta keep him alive until they get here. Keep breathing for him, Plenty, and I'll keep his heart pumping. It's all we can do right now."

Plenty nodded and bent again, placing her mouth over the weathered, wrinkled lips of the old Indian. "Please," Joey heard her whisper. "Please be strong. Don't die. I love you, Great- grandfather. I love you."

* * *

The hospital corridor was quiet as late afternoon

135

shadows caressed the flowered wallpaper and framed pictures on the walls. Somewhere, in the distance, the staccato beep . . . beep . . . beep of a machine announced that a patient's heart was still operating normally.

Occasionally a phone rang. Quiet voices spoke and footsteps echoed down the long passageway as doctors, nurses, and visitors passed one another, each lost in separate concerns.

Plenty sat with her chin resting on the smooth, metal railing that encircled the bed like a fence, keeping the sleeping form safely centered under the covers.

A series of red and yellow lights moved silently across the shiny face of an instrument beside the bed, recording the heartbeat, breathing rate, blood pressure, and temperature of the patient. A plastic bottle hung overhead, sending drips of clear liquid down a tube and into the man's arm.

The girl remained motionless. She'd been sitting there for hours, ever since the nurses had brought her great-grandfather up from the emergency room three floors below.

Everyone else had left to get a bite to eat in the cafeteria. Plenty didn't even know where it was. She didn't care.

The doctor had explained everything. Red Stone had suffered a heart attack, a "massive" one. A clot had cut off the flow of blood to one of the chambers in his heart, causing that part of the muscle to die. Lack of oxygen had done damage elsewhere, too.

Muscles scattered about the old man's body had been starved of the life-giving gas. Her great-grandfather would never be the same again. Someone would have to care for him night and day.

Plenty had spoken with her mother and father on the phone earlier. They'd offered to come as soon as they could get off work, but the girl had assured them that everything that could be done was being done. Red Stone was out of danger.

She and he would return to the reservation when his condition was stable enough for him to travel. Plenty understood that jobs were hard to come by for her people and that it was best, under the circumstances, for her parents not to take on his care. They must keep their bosses happy and not jeopardize their small but steady incomes.

Joey appeared at the door and leaned against the frame. "How's he doin'?"

Plenty nodded. "OK, still."

The boy let his gaze fall on the sleeping form. "I'm sorry he got sick. Really I am."

"I know," Plenty said. Then she added, "You saved his life. That's what the doctor said. He said you kept him from dying."

"*We* did," the boy urged. "We both did."

Plenty laid her chin back against the railing. After a long moment she spoke. "Why do things have to happen? You know. Bad things?"

The boy understood the question included a lot more than Red Stone's heart attack. Plenty's words came from deep in her heart, where hurt and hate lived.

"Just life, I guess," Joey sighed. "Bad things happen to everyone." He sat down in an empty chair. "But he's going to be OK. We'll take care of him. We can bring him to Freedom Mountain each summer and he can tell us stories—"

"No," Plenty interrupted. "He can't. He'll be too . . . too tired."

Joey nodded. "Then we'll come visit him. Summers just wouldn't be the same without your great-grandfather. He's my friend. We all love him very much."

The girl closed her eyes. "He talks about you often. Even back at the reservation, he's always telling me how well Joey rides the big black horse and how funny Wendy is and how much he likes Debbie's smile. I'd be jealous, 'cept I understand."

The girl reached over and stroked the man's cheek. "'A true warrior loves all people,' he'd tell me. That's what he wanted me to be, a warrior, a brave, strong—"

Tears slipped down Plenty's dark cheeks. "But I refused. I just wouldn't let myself be that kind of person."

Joey gazed at the old man sleeping on the pillow, his wrinkled face surrounded by thin strands of white hair. "Red Stone loves the mountains," he said quietly. "He can tell you the song of every bird and the call of every animal. There's something in the mountains and valleys that can change a person. Grandpa Hanson says the Creator God put it there, and I believe him. It changed me, forever.

138

Maybe it can change you, too."

The boy sighed. "We'd better go, Plenty. We'll come back tomorrow, first thing. OK? Doctor said Red Stone should rest now."

Plenty nodded and stood. Moving to the head of the bed, she bent and kissed the withered cheek of the man. "Good night, Great-grandfather," she whispered. "I'll be back tomorrow."

Joey smiled as the two teenagers slipped from the room, leaving the old Indian alone as the last rays of the sun faded, and the lights of the city blinked on.

* * *

"Are you all right?" Wrangler Barry walked over to the girl who stood in the moonlight, looking down at the sparkling waters below.

Debbie nodded. "I'm OK. Just thinking about Red Stone and Plenty. It's so sad."

Barry leaned against the railing. "Yeah, I know. Tough break. I like the old man."

The two were silent for a long moment, then the horseman spoke. "Debbie, there's something I've been meaning to talk to you about. Do you have a minute?"

"You're not going to yell at me for interfering in your life again, are you?" the girl said, a hint of coolness in her voice. "I've been trying to stay out of your way all summer."

Barry tapped his cane on the wooden supports holding them above the creek. "That's what I want to talk to you about. I mean, I want you to know that . . . oh, I'm not very good at saying things from inside."

Debbie worked a splinter free from the railing and tossed it into the creek. "You mean you *have* an inside?"

"OK, I deserve that. I haven't been very good company since the accident."

The girl nodded. "I miss the old Barry Gordon," she said, "the one who laughed at me all the time and made me feel like I was 9 years old."

"You liked that?"

"It was better than nothing."

Barry sighed. "I just didn't want to think of you as older because . . ."

"Because?"

"Because you're beautiful and wise and caring. You made my heart do stupid things."

Debbie turned. Barry noticed how the moonlight touched her cheek and shone through the carefully combed strands of her dark hair.

"I'm just a cowboy. I don't know fashion and high society and all that New York stuff. That was bad enough. Now I can't even ride a horse. As Joey would say, 'I ain't got nothin' goin' for me 'cept my incredible good looks and endless charm.' I'm not too sure about those, either."

Debbie grinned. "The charm could use a little work, but you aren't too shabby in the looks department. In fact, I think you're kinda cute, in a horse-about-to-have-a-foal sorta way."

"Yeah?"

"Yeah."

Barry shook his head. "Wait. Now I'm gettin' off the track. I just want you to know that . . . well . . . I'm sorry for being so cold to you this summer. I mean, here I was tellin' Alex how to accept himself and I was going around with a giant chip on my shoulder—"

"Beam."

"What?"

Debbie pointed at the young man's face. "*Beam in your eye.* That's what Grandpa Hanson would call it. It's in the Bible."

"Yeah . . . well . . . so here I have this beam in my eye and I can't see how lucky I am to have someone like you who wants to be around me even though I can't do stuff anymore like I used to and I guess what I'm trying to say is that I need you to—"

The horseman felt lips press against his, shutting off his rambling words. Arms gently encircled him as the creek sang its sweet song below his feet.

After what seemed like a very long time, he felt the pressure ease and stood looking into the soft eyes of the girl. "What were you saying, cowboy?"

Barry blinked. "I . . . um . . ." He smiled and touched her cheek. "I think I was about to say that . . . I love you."

Debbie grinned. "See? You're not as dumb as you think."

The two stood facing each other as the moon continued its journey across the night sky. Debbie's heart sang with the music of the waters. Now she knew her cowboy would be OK, as long as she was there to hold his hand and fill his life with hope.

* * *

Dawn was still an hour away when Joey drifted from sleep and opened his eyes. His first thoughts were about Plenty and the pain she was feeling. All her anger and hate had been masked by the terrible events of the day before. Would they return, this time only stronger? Would she ever stop blaming him and all other White people for robbing her great-grandfather of his mountain heritage?

Joey got up and slipped into his work clothes. He walked slowly from the barn just as the sky began to blush beyond the distant mountains.

Entering the Station, he ambled into the den, his mind searching for answers. What could he do to change the way Plenty looked at the world, her world? What could he say?

Sure, he'd been there to help save her great-grandfather. But they'd be returning to the reservation soon. Plenty would live among daily reminders of what other White people had done in the past. Every time she gazed at the mountains she'd be reminded that her people were once free to roam the hills and valleys, to hunt amid the peaks.

He saw Wendy sitting curled up with her ever-present photo album, the one she and David had produced during the summer. Joey smiled. That girl was always up before anyone else stirred.

"Hey, Wendy," he called quietly.

The girl blinked. "Well, Mr. Dugan. Is it noon already?"

Joey chuckled. "Couldn't sleep. Kept thinking about Plenty."

Wendy nodded. "Yeah. I know what you mean." She sighed. "Maybe you can talk to her some more when she gets back."

"Gets back? Whatta ya mean?"

"She left. About 20 minutes ago. Took one of the horses. Didn't think you'd mind."

Joey's brow furrowed. "Where'd she go?"

"I don't know. Rode down the drive and headed that way." The girl pointed. "Maybe she just needed to think for a while."

Joey scratched his head. "But she's sad. She shouldn't be all alone. What if she gets lost or confused?"

Wendy shrugged. "Maybe you should try to find her. She did look kinda tired and all. I would be, too, if my great-grandfather was bad sick."

The young horseman nodded. "Think I will. Tell your dad I'll be back as soon as I find her."

Wendy watched as Joey trotted down the steps and hurried across the lawn. He gave a short whistle and Tar Boy galloped over to meet him at the gate. Soon they were moving through the half light of dawn away from the Station in the direction of Freedom Mountain.

The trail became clearer and clearer as the eastern sky continued to brighten, transforming the horizon from a dark, amber hue to a lighter yellow. Tar Boy's hooves clattered over the stones and soil as the big animal carried his rider higher, higher, higher into the mountains.

What would he find once they reached the cave? He was sure that's where Plenty had gone. Would she greet him with arrow feathers poised at her cheek? What would he say to her? It couldn't go on anymore. The deep hatred in her heart had to stop. It just had to. She'd need her full energies to care for the old man who lay in the hospital bed in Bozeman.

Just before emerging from the tree line that surrounded Red Stone's cave, Joey reigned in his horse and slipped to the ground. Slowly he pushed back the branches that guarded the clearing.

As the first rays of the sun arched across the sky, Joey saw a movement at the cave entrance. A form stood, arms raised. Through the cold, mountain air a voice called in a language he couldn't understand.

As the morning chased the shadows away, Plenty's tear-stained face turned toward the rising sun, her determined smile greeting the brilliant light.

Joey paused, not sure of what was happening. As he watched, the girl's voice rose in strength until her strange words echoed through the forests and meadows, filling the mountaintop with sound.

Suddenly, he understood. Red Stone would never again come to his mountain. But his heart, the heart of the warrior, would continue to beat strong and true within the young girl who stood at the mouth of the cave, welcoming the new day.